What's the point in gaining the world

if we lose our souls?

To Emma

Best wishes
... and pleasant dreams!

3-7-11

BRYONY PEARCE

ANGEL'S FURY

EGMONT

EGMONT

We bring stories to life

Angel's Fury
First published in Great Britain 2011
by Egmont UK Limited
239 Kensington High Street
London W8 6SA

Text copyright © 2011 Bryony Pearce

The moral rights of the author have been asserted

ISBN 978 1 4052 5135 8

1 3 5 7 9 10 8 6 4 2

www.egmont.co.uk

A CIP catalogue record for this title is available from the British Library

Typeset by Avon DataSet Ltd, Bidford on Avon, Warwickshire
Printed and bound in Great Britain by the CPI Group

To Andy, Maisie and Riley

CONTENTS

PART ONE

INCEPTION

'Lord of the Universe, did we not warn You that man would prove unworthy of Your world?'

Chapter One
NIGHTMARES

Before my back hit the headboard I slammed on the sidelight. The bulb illuminated every corner of the room. There were no riflemen at the doorway.

I'm alive.

I grappled with the sweat-soaked sheets that were knotted around my legs, and once free I rocked back and forth, desperately trying to breathe through the pain.

People say you can't die in your dreams . . . they're wrong.

Finally I slumped down with my hands lying limp over the phantom bulletholes that riddled my chest.

After a moment I took a shuddering breath and fumbled my book from the bedside table. I didn't need to find my place – I'd read it a dozen times. The important thing was how fast I could be lost in the story; how far I could be pulled out of my own head.

As I read my eyes grew heavy but I resisted the tug of sleep. Zillah was lurking in the shadows ready to draw me into the field and I didn't want to go back. I glanced at the clock: 1.06.

Five hours till morning.

The men won't stop to let us clean up Amos's sick.

It oozes into the grooves beneath our shoes and the smell mixes with the reek of petrol until I feel sick too. I swallow and cover my mouth.

Daddy squeezes my knee. His face is white, so I cuddle closer to him.

Amos is sitting across from me. Our knees bump and I catch his eye, hoping he might play I-Spy for a bit, but he starts to gag.

I pull my legs back. 'Daddy, Amos is going to be sick again.'

Daddy jumps to his feet and bangs on the partition but the driver won't speak to him.

With my toes I prod the satchel that contains my most precious things. The picture of Mother is on top and I wonder if I should check that it's still clean. Amos gulps and covers his mouth.

We've been driving for almost two hours now. When are we going to stop?

Don't make me go through this again.

The thought pulled me out of the girl, but I stayed inside the dream and was forced to watch the trucks draw up to the field, a detached observer.

'I have to wake up, please, please, please.'

It was no good. I snapped back into the little Jewish girl.

Amos jumps up as soon as the engine stops. He knocks my knees to the side and runs to the back of the truck. But before he can stick his head through the tarpaulin it opens from the outside and the men are there.

They glare at us with mean eyes and Amos staggers back to his seat with his hands over his mouth.

The youngest of them gestures. 'Raus, dreißig Minuten Pause.'

I don't like the men, but I'm happy to be getting a break.

Daddy lets Amos and his family out ahead of us then he helps me on to the road. He stands next to me as I clutch my satchel and blink in the bright sunshine. Then my eyes adjust and I see a field of gold right next to us. After being stuck in the truck all morning it's tempting.

Daddy catches me as I start towards the barley. 'Stay by my side, Zillah,' he murmurs.

I hold in a sigh and watch the other trucks empty until around twenty of us are standing by the side of the road. I wave at my singing teacher. She looks away sadly.

The horrible men point to the field. 'Los dort entlang, da gibt es Mittagessen.'

I check Mother's watch. It's early for lunch and I'm not hungry, not even for my sweets, but everyone else starts to go where we're told so Daddy and I have to follow.

A couple of the younger children start to run around, but Daddy keeps hold of my hand. Some of the women sit and spread their skirts. Then they turn their faces to the sun. They remind me of flowers . . . so pretty. I look up as well and smile as the breeze sweeps away the memory of the awful journey. Birds wheel overhead. They make me feel dizzy so I look back down.

In the distance two hills create a deep valley. Standing exactly between them I face a schloss that hunches between the hills like an old chaperone. I almost giggle but my stomach rumbles, surprising me. We didn't eat this morning; we didn't have time. Maybe I could manage lunch after all.

I look for the men.

* * *

Irresistibly I floated upwards again.

'For God's sake . . . run!'

I shouted so loudly my throat hurt, but the girl didn't hear. She never runs . . . until it's too late.

'Please let me wake up before I . . .'

My singing teacher falls into the mud. Her skirt crumples and she looks into the sun with the new eye in the middle of her forehead.

I can't scream. My mouth won't work.

Some of Daddy's friends are running towards the trucks, but they keep being knocked back and the air fills with crimson rain, the crackle of gunfire and endless screaming.

My friend Amos falls next to his mother. His brother, Isaac, crawls towards us with blood all over his face.

Daddy shakes me and my head snaps back. 'Zillah, run!' He's wheezing. 'Get deep into the field and hide.'

Why does he sound so strange?

I stare at him. He's holding his arm and his hand is red.

'Daddy!' I reach up to touch him but he shoves me away. I burst into tears, drop my satchel and start to run.

I'm crying and coughing. Yellow dust chokes me and the barley stalks are taller than my head. I can hardly see. Daddy keeps his hand on my back and pushes me on.

Then, over all the noise, I hear him grunt. His hand falls from my back and the sun catches my face. His shadow isn't over me any more. I turn and find him face down on a line of grain.

My heart stops beating as it breaks.

Then the gunfire stops. It leaves behind a sickening silence. I struggle to see through the barley as the terrible men move into the field. Some of them are carrying shovels.

I crouch next to Daddy and shove my fingers in my mouth. I mustn't make a sound.

Then I hear Isaac's voice. He's begging. He invokes the name of God but the men ignore him. The sound of the gun going off is like the crack of ice on the winter river.

I shut my eyes.

The barley rustles right beside me, but I keep my eyes squeezed tight. I don't want to see the man who has come for me.

But there is no other noise and after a while I have to look.

One of them is standing above me, looking down with a half smile on his face. He is young. My lips tremble hopefully.

'Da bist du also Mäuschen,' he says.

Then he raises his gun.

As I staggered into the bathroom I knocked my elbow on the doorframe. Wincing and rubbing my arm I narrowed my eyes at the mirror. Today of all days I'd wanted to look halfway decent, but my hair was snarled into straggly knots and a deep itch on my forehead warned me a spot was on its way.

That's just great.

I stepped into the shower where I held my head under the hot water for as long as I could. As streams flowed between my toes I half dozed. Then I shook myself awake, washed my hair and dried off with one of Dad's towels. It went round me twice.

I've lost more weight.

My face swayed in the steamy mirror and for one confused moment I thought Zillah had broken out of my dreams. Quickly I wiped the glass. The long wet hair could be Zillah's, but the eyes looking back at me were grey, not brown and the face was older and ravaged by tiredness.

I fumbled with my concealer and tried to cover the red

blotches that flowered on my skin. Then I rubbed the stick back and forth under my eyes where the bags were nearly as dark as my pupils.

Pale as the dead I stared at myself: at my narrow, pinched lips, my long straight nose, the straggles of hair that wrapped around my shoulder.

Then I groaned and went to get dressed.

In the kitchen I reached for the coffee. Mum stopped laying out the breakfast things long enough to knock my hand away. 'You know I don't like you drinking that stuff.'

I tightened my ponytail and let her see my bloodshot eyes.

'Oh, Cassie.' Her shoulders slumped and she slid her own drink towards me. 'The exams are in a couple of months . . . after that it'll get better.' But she didn't meet my gaze. Instead she pulled on the cord of her gown and rubbed her slippers on a patch of faded lino as if to buff it up.

Yeah, right. I've had these nightmares as long as either of us can remember.

She looked up hopefully. 'Did you read that book?'

I wrapped my hands round the mug and nodded.

'She's an expert. I thought it might have the answer.' Her eyes dimmed. 'It didn't help, did it?'

I shook my head. 'No, it didn't.'

The book, *Learn Lucid Dreaming* by Leaza Ashworth MD, was in my wastebasket. I'd hurled it there this morning as soon as I'd got out of bed.

According to Doctor Ashworth I should be able to rewrite and redirect my own dream scripts: *CHANGE negative dream dimensions into their opposite, positive sides.* There was even an example: *If someone is trying to shoot you, replace that gun with flowers or give them a hug. If that proves too difficult, make the gun misfire, or the bullets whizz overhead.*

Pain throbbed round my heart, where the last bullet had ended Zillah's life.

Some expert!

Mum touched my hand and I jerked. Coffee slopped over my knuckles.

'Sorry, love.'

I didn't know if her apology was for the coffee or the book, but I grabbed a cloth from the cupboard under the sink and wiped the table before it could leave a mark.

'Have you brought your bags down?' Mum glanced into the hallway.

I nodded as I snagged a slice of toast from the grill.

'Good, your dad'll drive you to the airport before work.'

I almost dropped my toast. 'I thought I was getting a taxi!'

Mum's knuckles whitened on a chair back. 'We can't afford a taxi. Eat your breakfast . . . he'll be down in a bit.'

'Great.' I sprawled on the chair and she half turned, unable to meet my eyes as footsteps sounded on the stairs.

A grunt heralded Dad's discovery of my bags. Then he entered the kitchen and the atmosphere crystallised.

Mum looked as if she was going to speak, but the pan on the hob boiled over. She leaped to lift it from the heat. 'Damn . . . that's the porridge.'

Drops continued to splash and sizzle on the ring, curdling the air with the stench of burnt milk. Mum swiped a towel over the mess and Dad tilted his head meaningfully.

I took the pan and turned to face him. If I had to be stuck with him in the car for an hour I had to try one more time. 'Dad . . . I know you don't want me to go to Germany, but I have to. I won't be able to do my history coursework properly if I don't.'

Dad said nothing.

'Miss Barnes explained the coursework system to you – I heard her.'

Impossibly, his face hardened further. 'This isn't something we can afford, Cassie . . . Maybe if you were doing better at school it would be worth it . . .'

'You are *such* an asshole.' I dumped the pan next to the sink and slammed the back door open with my palm. The strains of next door's radio wafted into the kitchen and I paused with my foot on the back step. 'I'm paying for most of this trip with the money I earned at the restaurant . . . And if you'd let me do German I'd be getting straight As.'

Dad rubbed his chin, raw from his recent shave. 'We talked about this, Cassie. History and the sciences will be more useful to you in the long run than a language you won't use outside the classroom.'

'It isn't fair. You can't complain if I'm not doing well in subjects you made me take.'

'Cassiopeia Farrier.' Mum dropped the tea towel in the sink. 'Apologise to your father.'

'No!' Rage washed over me, red hot, and I glowered at the

veins of crimson that bled through Dad's pot-hemmed begonias. 'I was looking forward to going to Germany and he's ruining it.' My voice broke and I bolted into the back garden. 'It's not as if I'm not trying at school. In case you haven't noticed, I'm not sleeping too well.'

Mum's voice was muffled by the closing door, but her words darted after me. 'You aren't being fair on your father. It's hard for him . . . seeing you like this.'

I barely heard his reply. 'Just leave her, Marie. I'll take her to the airport – but I still think it's a mistake.'

CHAPTER TWO

HOPFINGEN

Forty of us trooped into Arrivals with snacks, iPods and Nintendos stuffed into our hand luggage. There we were bombarded by the sound of a language we couldn't understand: the tannoy boomed like a surf-sucked cave, local families chattered and the staff at passport control gossiped gutturally over our heads as they checked our photos.

The others were uneasy, even the GCSE German class. The boys remained in a tight band by thieving one another's passports; the girls huddled together more obviously. Some of them glanced at the duty-free shop, but none moved towards the cut-price cosmetics.

Yet as soon as the language entered my own ears I felt comfortable. My old German teacher, Miss Barnes, caught my eye and grinned as Mr Greene herded the group through the sliding doors and out to the car park. 'Nicola, I know you have a new phone and if it gets stolen because you're flashing it about you'll only have yourself to blame. Put it away. Now. Carl, leave Jess alone. Darren and Caroline let go of one another. Everybody outside.'

I didn't know why, but it was like coming home.

The air between the exit and car park, however, was humid and heavy. Gasping in the stifling atmosphere I pushed my way to the front of the line and was first on to the coach. I found a seat halfway down the aisle and, knowing no one else would want to sit there, dumped my bag next to me. Then I leaned on the window and blanked out my classmates.

The driver gunned the engine and a thrill went through me: I couldn't wait to see what Germany really looked like. But as we passed one dull high-rise after another disappointment chilled my cheeks.

Is this it? We might as well have gone to Milton Keynes.

The glaring signs were all too familiar: Coca-Cola, Accenture, Toyota. Miserably I closed my eyes.

The seat prickled my bare legs and I fidgeted uncomfortably before I looked out through the smeared glass again.

Now trees spotted the roadside and structures were growing more suburban. On signs German words began to stand out: directions to the town centre and swimming baths. But the buildings leaned on a skyline that had darkened to the colour of an ageing bruise.

A storm's coming. Can we outrun it?

As if in response to my thought the coach speeded up and we quickly turned off the Autobahn into quieter, narrower roads. Here the greenery increased, almost blocking my view of the wounded sky.

The driver switched on a local radio station and I glanced at my watch. We'd been driving for forty minutes. A European rock song, made even more incomprehensible by the DJ's chatter, crackled out through the speakers.

The boys jeered and I heard the driver speak crossly to Miss Barnes. He only had a tape player; he couldn't play Sticky's Killers CD even if he wanted to.

I turned back to the window. We had finally abandoned the city. Fields slid by in a kaleidoscope of green and yellow sunlight my eyelids turned to lead and m...

with a sting of m... ...he curtain near my forehead and ...ave been buzzing from the double espresso

I'd managed to snag at Stansted, I couldn't muster the energy to brush it away.

Violently I shook my head and forced my arms towards my bag. Originally I'd had a plastic fork in the front pocket, but it had been confiscated at Security, so I'd have to make do with a hairclip.

I gnawed the little plastic tags off the end then checked that no one was watching. When I was sure that I remained invisible, I ground my teeth and scratched the top of my thigh with the metal spoke.

Immediately a welt appeared, but it was worth it: the pain cleared the rising fog from my head.

I mustn't fall asleep in front of everyone. If I have the nightmare here, everyone will know what a freak I am.

Clutching the hairgrip in one hand and the handle of my bag

The other I tried to keep my head upright . . . but it kept lolling.

of the gun . . . ty metal reminded me of blood and the image

I jabbed my leg b . . . . . . wam into my mind's eye. Frantically

to feel it.

The storm clouds made . . . wood. I was too far *gone*

. . . ing

movement of the coach was too strong to fight. I realised my head was resting on the window.

How did that happen?

One last coherent thought jittered through my mind.

Maybe we'll get to Hopfingen before I start to dream . . .

Daddy shuts the gate. He makes me stand with our neighbours and I hug my satchel so tightly that the frame of Mother's picture digs into my chest.

The men watch us closely and their cold eyes make me shiver. When they see Daddy lock up behind us, they nod, as if he's done something good.

I don't understand why we're leaving our home and all our things. I try to complain, but Daddy digs his fingers into my shoulder and I know I must be silent.

We walk through the town, passing the tall houses with their curtains closed against us. The baby, Maria, squawks and her mother, Dinah Heidler, shushes her nervously.

Ahead of us the town square opens up. I see many of our friends there already, all with luggage, just like us.

A strained clonking sounds across the square. It comes from the white clock tower that rises above the fountain. The bells don't work, but you can still hear it trying to strike the hour. It's sort of sad.

As the clock quietens, Daddy gives me a gentle push, reminding me to keep moving. Soon we reach the base of the fountain and I look into the stone eyes of the Lady. Her arms are full of hops and her hair covers her dress. One day my hair will be that long. She is lifting one foot, as if to test the water at her feet. I've sat on her stone seat almost every day of my life. I wonder if I'll ever sit there again.

A bell jangles and I look up. Fräulein Ehrlichmann, who owns the sweet shop, has come out to sweep her step. I see her notice us then rush back inside.

Sadness is a weight on my chest. I like her sweets. I don't understand why people are being so unkind.

Then the bell chimes once more and Fräulein Ehrlichmann runs across the street. One of the men tries to hold her up, but she shoulders past him and comes to stand in front of me. There's a paper bag in her hand.

'Here.' She hands it to me and I feel the hidden lumps.

Humbugs! A whole bag.

Fräulein Ehrlichmann turns to Daddy. 'They say you're going somewhere better. You'll be with your own kind.' She touches her *shiny yellow curls. 'This'll be good for everyone, you'll see.'*

Daddy grunts and she strokes my black hair with her red fingers.
'Goodbye, Zillah.'

Then the trucks pull up.

Fräulein Ehrlichmann rushes away and does not look back.

I jerked awake and slowly opened my aching hand. The hairclip
was pressed into my palm so deeply I had to peel it free.

My heart hammered; before today my dreams had been as
predictable as my arguments with Dad. Every night I relived
Zillah's death. Sometimes I saw it from different viewpoints or
joined it at different places, but as far as I could remember I'd
never dreamed anything else.

Until now.

And although the dream had been tame by my standards, it
had left me deeply disturbed.

Probably because I know what happens once Zillah gets on
that truck.

Furtively I wiped my chin with my wrist. No one was com-
menting on my behaviour, so I must have managed to sleep quietly
. . . for a change. I forced my shoulders to relax into the seat and

looked out of the window just in time to see the sign that welcomed us to Hopfingen.

The coach stopped outside the *Jugendherberge* and the doors hissed open like airlocks. Bag in hand I stood and slipped into the aisle ahead of my classmates.

As I passed the driver I heard a strangely familiar clonking sound and stopped. My eyes swivelled to a white tower that glowed against the sky above the youth hostel. The clock was trying to strike three, but it couldn't, because the mechanism didn't work.

The blood drained from my face and I froze, one foot on the top step, as petrified as the statue I was suddenly certain I would find in the town square.

'C'mon, Farrier, move it.' A hand shoved me in the centre of my back and I stumbled down the steps. Only Mr Greene's palm stopped me from falling and grazing my knees on the cobbles.

Trancelike, I stepped towards the open road. I had to see that square. But Mr Greene caught hold of my arm. 'There'll be time for exploring later, Cassie. Listen to Miss Barnes.'

I tried to tune in to the orientation talk, but my mind kept spinning to the broken clock in the white tower. In the corner of

22

my eye I could just see it, slightly taller than the circling houses, tantalisingly near.

I tried to remember whether or not Miss Barnes had shown us a picture of Hopfingen before we left, but so many of my lessons were a blur of exhaustion that I couldn't say for sure.

Suddenly my attention was reined back; the girls were clinging to one another with little squeals. I shook my head, feeling as if my ears were filled with water. Miss Barnes was saying something important.

'. . . So you need to pair up. There are a couple of rooms with three beds. Yes, Jess, your little threesome can have one of them.' She rattled her clipboard and continued. 'One group of girls and one group of boys can have a room with three beds, everyone else find a partner and we'll go into the hostel.'

The question of the strange clock tower was banished by a more urgent horror.

If I have to share a room, I won't be able to switch on the light in the middle of the night. When I wake up I'll have to stay alone in the dark.

Fear stuck my tongue to the roof of my mouth. I'd been lucky on the bus: the new dream had allowed me to sleep quietly. But

23

what were the chances I'd get away with that tonight?

Tomorrow everyone's going to know just how weird Cassie Farrier really is.

I panicked silently as the girls paired up until only three were left. The small group clutched one another and looked at me as if I was toxic waste.

I clenched my teeth and waited to see who would lose the lottery.

'Izzy, Fran and Nicola, one of you has to pair up with Cassie.' Mr Greene left my side and marched over to the dithering trio. 'Come on, or I'll make the choice for you.'

'Mr Greene, *please*, two of us can share a bed.'

My heart rose at their suggestion then fell again when I saw the expression on Mr Greene's face.

'Don't be ridiculous. Right, that's it. Nicola, let go of Fran's arm and stand by Cassie.'

Mr Greene cast an aggrieved look in my direction.

Like it's my fault none of the others want to share with me.

The youth hostel was a tall building and Nicola and I had the room at the very top. When we got inside, though, I forgot about the difficult climb in my rush to look through the window.

My fingers tightened on the sill. From here I could see the white clock tower in the town square quite clearly and, just as I had dreamed, there was a fountain underneath. My eyes locked on to the monument and my fingernails cracked on the gloss.

The Lady stood in the single shaft of light that broke through the clouds. Her dress was immortalised in the moment of falling from her shoulder and her arms were packed with bronzed hops. She hadn't changed since Zillah had seen her for the last time. My breath caught.

What's happening to me?

Nicola shouldered me aside to see the view for herself and my knees collapsed as soon as my legs hit the bed.

'The storm's starting,' she said.

Not wanting to speak to her I fumbled in my bag for my earphones and managed to shove them in place just as the first flurry of rain battered the window.

We had the afternoon free, but as no one wanted to brave the downpour we were allowed to stay inside until it cleared. At four the sky turned a stunning cobalt blue and the clouds vanished, leaving only slicks of glistening puddles behind them.

We gathered in front of the building.

'Here are your maps. Don't forget to be polite and respectful to the locals. If I receive any complaints the offender will be sent home on the next plane.' Miss Barnes handed out information packs. 'German class: please practise your phrases as much as possible. Nicola, that means you, pay attention please. History class: see which of these monuments you can find. Everyone back here at five thirty.'

Nicola immediately rushed off with her friends and I shoved the bundle of paper into my back pocket without looking at it. I knew where I wanted to go: I had to see the fountain up close.

Soon I realised I wasn't the only one heading to the square. When I saw that most of the class were following I stomped angrily on the cobbled road.

'Out the way, loser.'

'Shove it, Sticky. Why don't you go somewhere else?'

He elbowed me off the pavement so he could hold hands with Caroline. 'There's a sweet shop down here, freak-face, we're all going in, so why don't you go and find a cemetery to lurk in.'

Gutter water seeped into my trainers and my mouth filled with the taste of the sausage I'd eaten at lunchtime.

Could the same shop still be there?

I broke into a run and overtook the others. I had to find out. The square opened in front of me and there it all was: the fountain with its stone seat, the clock tower . . . and the sweet shop. Some things had changed enough that the dream image was no longer quite accurate, but it was clearly the same place.

The shop sign was now faded and cracked across the middle and the window was jammed with jars of boiled sweets, jelly shapes, pyramids of homemade chocolates, wooden figures, steins and pictures of local landmarks – very different from the rainbow of orderly glass jars that Zillah had known.

A rusting bell dangled from a spring above the door and it rang irritably again and again as my classmates disappeared inside. I watched, stunned, then lurched across the *Platz* like a zombie.

When my knees bumped the fountain I looked into the Lady's heavy-lidded eyes and goosebumps stippled my forearms. A few hours ago she had watched me . . . no – Zillah . . . climb into the truck for her final journey.

This close I could see that, like the sign above the sweet shop, she had in fact aged. Her face was weather-worn and one of her arms was damaged. The remains of dark orange graffiti were daubed on her stone seat and deeply etched declarations of love, irremovable and aged with green moss, decorated the rim like clumsy filigree. The air rushed out of me and I slumped down without a care for the hearts and arrows beneath my legs.

Splashes of water cooled the scratches on my thigh and I reached a trembling finger to touch the Lady's toe, half convinced she had to be an illusion. My fingertip met solid rock.

I snatched my hand back and cradled it. Then I waited for the shop to empty.

By the time the bulk of my classmates had left the square the vile flavour of almost-sick had faded from my tongue.

Around me curtains began to twitch and, like villagers shocked to have survived an invasion, the Germans cracked open windows and emerged from their bolt-holes. Female tones launched into full gossip mode and I hunched my shoulders, feeling like a foreigner for the first time.

I scuttled to the shop and stopped as the door burst open.

Sticky and Caroline cannoned on to the pavement, giggling.

One of his hands was on the back of her shirt and the other was inside his jacket pulling out a Snickers bar.

'Sticky, you're so *bad*.' Caroline extended the last word, rolling it round her mouth like a chocolate.

My eyes widened. 'Did you steal that?'

Sticky glowered. 'Tell everyone, why don't you, Vampira.' He handed the chocolate to his girlfriend. 'Here, babe, for you.'

'You're pathetic,' I snapped, but I was forced to step sideways to let them past.

'Whatever, anorexia girl, don't know why you're going in there – it's obvious you don't eat anything.' Caroline tossed her shiny mane and pouted at my legs. 'C'mon, Sticky, let's go to the river.' They bundled past and knocked me into the windowsill.

My lip curled as I watched them go, then my gaze fell on a set of initials carved into a niche beneath my wrist and I instantly forgot all about them. I brushed the stone with a frown. The letters were well worn, but I could make them out: K. F.

My lip trembled. The graffiti on the fountain hadn't affected me, but these initials felt important somehow.

I need to know why I'm dreaming about a place I've never seen.

Filled with determination I opened the door and the bell rattled as I stepped across the threshold.

Before I had a chance to take in the crowded shelves, a tiny brunette popped up from behind the counter. '*Guten Tag. Kann ich dir helfen?*'

I dredged my memory to come up with a polite response. '*Danke schön, schaue mich nur um.*' I am just looking. I had to apologise for my stilted German. '*Es tut mir leid. Ich bin Engländerin.*'

'*Ach du kommst aus England.* Your German is very good; you have a lovely accent. Very local. You have been listening well to us speak, yes? Welcome to my shop. Tell me if you need anything.'

I stared blindly at the sweets laid out on the counter, unable to even consider the taste of sugar on top of my sour stomach.

Then my eyes lifted from a jar of bright candy letters to a faded black-and-white picture that hung above the counter.

In the portrait the sweet shop sign was new and the blonde woman I had seen in my dream was standing on the front step. Her face was drawn into a tight smile and her hands were clenched on a jar of sweets as if she was afraid someone would take them from her.

'W-who's that?'

The shopkeeper appeared by my elbow and a blast of Fisherman's Friends scalded my cheek as she breathed over me. 'It is my great-aunt Karla – this was her shop. She lives upstairs now and she still keeps safe the best recipe for the truffles.'

'Your . . . great-aunt Karla?'

'Yes. This was taken just before the war. How pretty she is, yes?'

I nodded, still staring at her blonde curls. 'K. F.? Is that her?'

Karla's niece snorted and gestured outside. 'Ha, *nein*. You mean the –' she paused, seeking the right word – 'graffiti on the wall outside? Yes?'

I nodded.

'My great-aunt is Karla Ehrlichmann. K. E., see? We'd have removed the letters, but the poor boy who made them, he died. I think his name was Kurt Faber. Aunt Karla had an –' she paused again and waved her fingers – 'affection for him. *Gummibären*?'

I had to grip the counter for support. 'What?'

'Gummi bears? Good, *ja*?'

I nodded and realised that she thought I'd been staring at a jar of the jewel-coloured jellies. 'Sure . . . thanks.'

The shopkeeper filled a white paper bag for me. 'I am Astrid,' she said suddenly. 'Astrid Kaufman.' She handed me the sweets. 'I hope you enjoy your stay in Hopfingen. One euro exactly, please.'

I fumbled in my wallet for the money then paused and reached for a second coin. 'My friend out there realised that he forgot to pay for something.'

Astrid looked at me steadily for a moment then took both euros. Soft fingers wrapped round my wrist and she reached under the counter. 'Here. For you.'

Three expensive handmade chocolates were placed into my palm.

'Don't tell your friends.' She winked and I looked at the chocolates. Each had a yellow star iced on top.

'*Danke schön*. Really.' I backed out of the shop, clutching the sweets.

I stood in the square beneath the Lady, chocolate melting in my hand.

I had no answers after all, only more questions. I thought of the faceless boy who had carved his initials beneath the sweet-shop window. He and Karla had been in love, at least I figured that was what Astrid had meant by *an affection*.

My gaze was drawn to the first floor of the sweet shop where a blue curtain flapped in the breeze. I knew there was an old woman in there, but in my mind's eye she was a young blonde, grieving for the loss of her lover. Had she traced his initials with her fingertips every time she left the building, trying to feel closer to him?

I couldn't help wondering about the boy too. Kurt Faber.

Sudden cold made me shiver and I crossed my arms over my chest.

CHAPTER THREE

DISCOVERY

The lights went out and Nicola was nowhere to be seen.

She's sleeping with her friends after all.

Relieved, I wilted against the bathroom sink. Tiredness made me ache all over, as if I had the flu, yet I was reluctant to lie down, dreading what I'd see when I closed my eyes.

Would it be Zillah's death again? The new dream set in the square? Or maybe something worse?

The new unpredictability of my nightmares terrified me. Now I had no way of preparing myself for what I would see.

Abruptly voices came from the stairs. 'Nicola, don't argue. Go to your own room. You can't sleep on the floor.'

I threw down my toothbrush, ran and dived under my duvet.

Just as the clock in the square was struggling to strike Nicola stomped into our room and tossed her wash bag on the night-stand. 'You did this, didn't you, freak? You told on me.'

Miss Barnes's voice came from the doorway. 'I'm sure I can work out what a lump on the floor means, Nicola, especially when you're whispering with your friends so loudly. Leave Cassie alone please. She's sleeping.'

I heard Nicola climb into bed and thump the pillow. She humphed a few times, as if wanting attention or an apology. I clenched my teeth; she'd get neither from me. After a few moments Miss Barnes sighed. 'I'll be patrolling the corridors tonight, Nicola, understand? Any more silliness and I'll be calling your mother.' She pulled the door closed behind her and I felt the force of Nicola's glare through my duvet.

Eventually she spoke. 'Are you awake?'

I made no reply, only clenched my fists under my chin. My whole body was wound tight as a spring, and I waited in silence until her breathing deepened.

Bile rose in my throat, pushed there by a spurt of jealousy that twisted my gut into knots.

How come Nicola Watson gets to sleep so easily while I get to relive Zillah's death night after night?

I glared into the darkness as I listened to her snore, too afraid to close my eyes.

Finally I tiptoed to the window. The cold air behind the curtain revived me, so I sat on the bench under the sill and pressed my cheek against the glass.

The stars shimmered through a web of cloud and my eye was drawn to Orion's Belt. It shone like a diamond bracelet, bright as I had ever seen, and my shoulders started to relax as I began the search for my very own constellation. When I found Cassiopeia glowing in its familiar place I inhaled. Across from the Plough, the crown seemed to pulse in the night sky, almost equal in brightness to Orion.

My breath fogged the window and I watched the stars glow until my sight blurred.

The teachers hadn't let me have coffee this evening so there was no caffeine in my system. My body needed oblivion and I had no way of fighting it. Slumber dragged me under like a current.

The polish on my jackboots cracks as I crouch beneath the window. It took me an hour this morning to bring up the shine, but I don't care.

My fingers rest lightly on the brick and I feel dizzy as my nose fills with the scent of sweets I cannot afford. I lean my forehead on my arm and listen to Karla humming as she works. This close, I imagine that I can smell her. Her scent always reminds me of candied almonds, as if she herself has a sugar coating.

Pressing my palm to the windowsill I think about last night and need her to know that I am close by. More, I want her to think of me every time she opens her door. A piece of slate grinds under my heel. I pick it up and start to dig into the wall beneath the sill. I will create a sign just for her.

As I finish the first letter of my name I hear the distinctive snap of a female voice and spin round, still crouching. The Jewish singing teacher is herding a group of her students across the square.

She casts a stern look in my direction and I clutch the stone tighter.

Finally the Jewess and her flock disappear round the corner. After a moment I frown at my wrist. Blood is dripping into my shirt sleeve. Painfully I open my fingers and release the stone. It thuds back to the ground.

I jerked awake and cracked my head on the windowpane. Shock made me cry out and I fell off the bench.

Nicola stirred and I swore under my breath as I stumbled back to bed.

Where were these new dreams coming from? Tears streamed down my face as I looked back at the window. I'd left the curtain hanging open and Orion blazed in the centre of the gap. I watched the sky until dawn gilded the ceiling and tried not to dwell on the fact that I might be losing my mind.

'Bayreuth today.'

'Um, yeah.' I frowned and pulled my jumper over my head.

Why's Nicola talking to me?

She cleared her throat. 'Look, I'm sorry about last night. I just wanted to sleep with my mates. You understand, right?'

'Sure . . .'

She came to stand in front of me. 'You know, you could do with more make-up; it would draw some attention away from those bags.' She waved her hand in my face and I ducked away. 'I could make you over if you like.'

She smiled and I narrowed my eyes. 'No offence, Nicola, but what do you want?'

'Fine.' She squared her shoulders. 'You're good at German, right?' I opened my mouth and she flicked her fingers. 'Yeah, I know, you dropped it. But you're still better than most of my class.' She spread her palms. 'Look, here's the thing. If I get above a C in my coursework, I get driving lessons. So I need some help.'

She showed me another over-sweet smile. 'I can give you make-up lessons in return.'

My lips twitched and Nicola sighed. 'Look, we're stuck in this room together so we might as well . . . you know . . . use each other.'

I sucked air between my teeth, ready to tell her where to get off. Then I caught a glimpse of us both in the full-length mirror behind her.

The sight made me close my eyes. '. . . Alright.'

She grinned. 'We'll start this evening, yeah?'

We'd been driving towards Bayreuth for an hour and were firmly into farming country when suddenly the hairs on my neck stood up. I ran my hand beneath my ponytail and my skin started to prickle. Sweat trickled down the inside of my jumper.

I spun in my seat, but my classmates were huddled at the rear of the bus craning to see something in Sticky's notebook. They couldn't be the source of the threat I sensed.

I tried to dismiss the eerie feeling, looked out of the window and almost jolted off my seat. We were driving past fields of hops and barley. Almost directly opposite, two hills created a deep

V-shaped valley and between them a schloss hunkered into the centre of the depression like an aged chaperone.

I've seen this view every night of my life.

My heart jumped madly and my hands flew to my mouth. Before I could stop it vomit sprayed the seat in front. I cupped my hands beneath my chin to protect my clothes and my classmates began to jeer.

Miss Barnes called for the driver to stop then swayed towards me as we creaked to a halt. She dug in her pocket for tissues and leaned on the back of the seat opposite.

'Here you go, Cassie.' As my classmates piled disgustedly off the bus, she dabbed my overflowing hands with a wad of tissue. 'I'll clean this up. Get some fresh air and make sure Mr Greene gives you a bottle of water.'

Abandoning my bag I slid shakily into the aisle. My chin and cheeks were wet. I had to wash my face, but had nothing I could use until I got off the bus and faced everyone.

I raised my head so I could see where I was going and the scene through the slewed front window struck me like a fist in the gut. We had stopped directly in front of the hill-hemmed barley field.

A sharp ache pulsed behind my right eye and my belly cramped again. I rushed off the bus and threw up at Mr Greene's feet.

Loud exclamations and girlish shrieks greeted this display and my face burned even as the blood tried to flee my cheeks.

Finally my stomach was empty and I nudged tacky strands of hair out of my face. Mr Greene gestured with a bottle of Evian and I held out my hands.

I cleaned myself up as best I could and swilled water around my mouth until the taste of regurgitated meat faded. Then I moved further from the bus to wipe my spattered legs.

When I was done I gathered my courage and turned to face the field.

My knees trembled and I rubbed my eyes, reasoning desperately.

We're less than an hour out of Hopfingen. In my dream Zillah drives for two hours – it can't be the same place.

But . . . those trucks wouldn't have travelled very fast.

I had to face it. This was the place Zillah had died. My classmates and I were standing at the site of a horrifying massacre.

'Cassie?'

A hand on my shoulder made me jump. It was Nicola.

'What do you want?' My voice was colder than I'd meant it to be.

The other girl stepped back, fumbled in her pocket and came out with an Airwaves. 'Here.' She dropped the pellet in my hand.

'Thanks.' I stared at her as I slid the gum into my mouth. Her phone was poking out of her jeans. 'Your phone . . .'

Nicola's fingers hovered protectively over her precious iPhone. 'What about it?'

'It has GPS, right?'

Suspicion tightened her features. 'Why?'

My mind raced. 'I-I just want to know how long we've got before we get to Bayreuth.' Nicola glanced back at her mates and I looked away. 'Never mind . . . if you don't know how to use it.'

'Don't be stupid.' Nicola tugged the phone free and I kept my face blank as her fingers danced across the screen. 'Here.' She waved it in front of me. 'It says we have another forty-five minutes.'

'So that's where we are . . . those coordinates?'

'Yes.' She whipped the phone away, but the information still danced in front of my eyes. I now knew exactly where we were.

Nicola huffed as she put her phone back in her pocket. 'I bet the bus stinks now.'

She loped back to her friends and I returned my gaze to the field. The sounds of my classmates faded away and I imagined the air filled with screams and the crackle of gunfire.

As I dropped my bag on my new seat I spotted my Meg Cabot jammed into the top of it and ran my fingers over the rumpled pages. *When Lightning Strikes* was about a girl able to find people through psychic visions.

What if this is something similar? If I'm some sort of . . . medium, then maybe there's a way I can end the dreams.

My hands tightened on the book.

These visions could be haunting me because Zillah's spirit wants the world to know what happened. My nightmares might go away if someone finds her body.

I stopped breathing, terrified of derailing my train of thought.

I could leave a tip with the police. I've got the coordinates of the field and I don't have to give my name. I've got nothing to lose.

My breath trembled as I made up my mind: I'd do anything to end the nightmares. When we got back to Hopfingen I'd find a payphone and first chance I got I'd leave a tip with the *Landespolizei.*

I fixed my eyes steadfastly on the field as the bus pulled away and said a silent farewell to the little Jewish girl I knew was buried there.

If this worked, I'd never have to see her again.

PART TWO

INCARNATION

'Filled with repentance for what his lust had unleashed Shemhazai asked the Lord if there was any hope for mankind . . . The Lord replied: "I will bind your sons into fleshly bodies for three hundred generations."'

Chapter Four

DISCLOSURE

My palm smacked into the touch lamp and it crashed on to the floor. The sound echoed the gunshots that still crackled in my ears.

I rested my head in my hands. I'd been home a week.

Maybe they haven't found the grave yet.

The old dream still haunted me. Its details were as vivid as ever, but each night a new variation ripped my rest apart.

I dug my knuckles into my eyes and checked the clock. I'd barely slept for an hour. Defeated, I lay back down and stared at the shadows on the wall, waiting for sleep to wash the next horror over me.

Unable to face eating, I pushed cornflakes around my bowl.

Mum bustled into the kitchen and started washing up. 'Did you hear the headlines? Shall I turn it up?'

'What?'

'The headlines.' She rolled her eyes at me and twiddled the

volume on the radio. 'They said something about our twin town, Hopfingen. You were there last week. Was anything going on?'

I shook my head and put down my spoon. As I waited for the news I gripped the work surface, my heart beating faster. The piece that mentioned Hopfingen was last. It had hit the international news, but wasn't as important as some celebrity's latest wardrobe crisis.

'The German town of Hopfingen has been rocked by reports of a mass grave less than sixty miles from its boundary. Some of the victims have now been identified as local residents whose records were never located at Flossenbürg Concentration Camp, where it was previously believed they had ended their lives.

Investigators are operating under the assumption that this is grisly evidence of a, till recently undiscovered, war crime. However, we understand that police were led to the grave by an anonymous tip and are keen to speak to the individual who left the information.'

If they've found the grave why haven't my nightmares gone?

'Cassie?'

'W-what happened?' I looked around, confused. I was on the

floor. I levered myself on to my elbows, skidded on cornflakes and slipped back down.

'You fainted.' Mum offered me a hand, but as she spoke my memory replayed the previous moments.

Oh, God, I'm never going to be free.

I curled into a ball among the remains of my breakfast and pressed my hands over my ears, trying to silence the news report that seemed to be playing on a loop in my head.

'Dave!' Mum shouted. 'Get down here.'

Dad's voice preceded him into the kitchen. 'What is it? I have to go.' His feet stopped in the doorway. 'What's wrong with Cassie?' I curled up tighter and Dad's wrist rested briefly on my forehead. 'She hasn't a temperature.' Mum murmured something and he pulled his hand away. 'I knew something like this would happen if we let her go to Germany.'

'There was no way to be sure. She had to go . . . It was about her future.'

'And this is about the past,' Dad growled.

I opened my eyes.

'We don't know that.' Mum clutched an RNLI tea towel as if it was a lifebelt.

Dad climbed to his feet and smoothed his suit. 'I need to call the office.'

'What?' Mum gave a little jump, like a rabbit caught out of its hole.

'I'm not going in today. We've got to sort this out. It's time she knew.'

'No!' Mum sounded desperate. 'We agreed it wouldn't help.'

Dad gestured towards me. 'You don't think it can make things any worse, do you?' His legs momentarily obscured my view of Mum as he moved to the kitchen door. 'I'm going for the video.'

'Can't we talk about this? Look at the state of her.'

'Get her into the front room, Marie. You've got time to calm her down a bit. I've got to get the VCR out of the loft and hook it up.'

'*Dave!*'

'We're doing this.' His voice broke. 'Ignoring it isn't working. How long has it been since she last slept? It's killing me that there's nothing I can do for her. I can't watch her fall apart like this any more.'

I didn't think he'd even noticed. I slid my slitted gaze towards his face; his expression was more determined than I'd ever seen it.

'Let's try telling her the truth.' He gripped the door frame and met Mum's eyes. 'If it doesn't help, we've always got that number.'

When Mum spoke I was shocked to hear her crying. 'We said we'd never use it again.'

Dad said nothing more; he simply made for the stairs. I heard him leave a short message for his office then the trapdoor banged above the landing. Mum stood still for a minute then laid the tea towel over the pooled milk and crouched next to me.

My head whirled.

What are they talking about? What 'truth' have they been hiding?

Mum shook my shoulder. 'Come on, Cassie. We're going to the front room. You can lie on the sofa. You aren't going to school today.'

I cradled a cup of coffee sweetened with four sugars. Mum hadn't even objected when I asked for it. Dad was bent behind the television, swearing as he swapped SCART leads. The old VCR sat at his feet, the buttons outlined in dust. He put the silver DVD player on the carpet next to it. Then he hefted the video recorder into place on the shelf. It fitted. The cabinet had once been designed for it, after all.

Dad looked at Mum and they both looked at me. Then he pulled a video box from his jacket. A business card was taped to the front, but I couldn't make out the faded lettering.

'Are you sure about this?' Mum winced.

Dad ran his hands through his greying hair. 'A picture speaks a thousand words.'

He slid the video into the slot. There was a mechanical whirring as the machine inhaled it and my fingers tightened on my cup.

'Cassie,' he said, 'put your coffee down.'

I placed the mug on the floor. For once I wasn't about to argue with him.

A picture shimmered into focus and Dad's face appeared.

The screen was a magic mirror, reversing the damage of the years. In this image Dad's hair was brown, his skin unlined. But his mouth formed a line above his jutting chin and he was aged by the shadows in his eyes.

This younger version swallowed and nodded at the person behind the camera. 'It's working?'

'You can start any time.'

That's not Mum's voice.

I leaned forward.

The Dad on screen ruffled his hair in a familiar gesture and looked away from the camera. 'I'm not sure we should be doing this,' he muttered.

'It's a good idea to make the recording, Mr Smith. Evidence is often essential in these cases.'

I frowned.

Our name's Farrier. Why did she call Dad Mr Smith?

I squinted across the room, but my parents weren't looking at me. Their eyes were fixed on the window into our past.

The conversation was continuing. Quickly I turned back and stared into the television.

'Okay,' Dad said. 'I'm Dave Smith and this video is being taken at –' he checked his watch – 'four p.m. on the thirtieth of June 1984. Um . . .'

'Go on.' There was a strangely familiar ring to the woman's voice, yet I was certain I'd never heard it before. I clenched my fists.

'My daughter, Cassie, is twenty-three months old. She's just started talking.' Dad stepped away from the camera to reveal a strange living room overrun with the detritus of life with a small child: an overturned doll's pram, a set of building blocks, a miniature chair and table covered with crayons and paper. 'You can come in now, Marie.'

The door opened and my mother came into view. She was walking backwards, but her step had a bounce in it that I didn't recognise. Her hair was pulled into a springy ponytail and when she glanced at the camera her chin was defined, her eyes bright.

She gestured to someone who remained outside the room. 'Come on, Cassie. Come on, pumpkin. Follow Mummy.'

I held my breath as the camera panned to show a child. She was confident on her feet, a toddler, but she still held her arms in front of her as if to prevent a fall that almost, but didn't quite happen. Her grey eyes, when she looked towards us, were huge in her chubby baby face and her hair was curled wispy brown around her ears.

Then those eyes widened and she stopped and bumped on to her bottom. Mum knelt beside her. 'It's alright, pumpkin, you remember Doctor Ashworth, don't you?'

Even through the grainy picture I could see the little girl's bottom lip tremble. She turned her head into her mother's shoulder and fisted her hands in her T-shirt.

Dad levered her off Mum with a nervous glance towards the camerawoman. 'Sorry. She's obviously going through a shy stage. Come on, pumpkin, it won't be for long. Just say a few words for the camera. Do it for Daddy.'

Mum scooped up a toy and my fingers twitched in recognition. Bunny still lived upstairs on the end of my bed.

On the television a game of Peekaboo was in progress. Finally the little girl showed her face again and giggled. 'Wo ist Bunny?'

As if in stereo, Mum and Dad, who were both watching the screen as avidly as a car crash, swallowed audibly.

I shook my head.

She isn't English. My God . . . I'm adopted. I'm German.

I glanced at Mum and she gestured towards the screen with a shake of her head. It wasn't finished.

The mum in the video placed Bunny in her daughter's hand. 'Here's Bunny.'

'Danke, Mama.' The little girl wrapped both arms round the ragged toy. 'Ich habe Hunger.'

'Here you are.' Mum lifted an apple from the bowl on the dresser.

'Nein, nein Mama. Das will ich nicht.' The child pushed the

fruit away and her face screwed up. Her shoulders hitched and Mum looked at the figure holding the camera with a panicked expression.

There was a slight movement as though the camerawoman had shrugged. 'She wants something else.'

Mum shook her head. 'No, baby, we're having tea in a little while.' She looked at the camera. 'I'd better take her outside. Is that enough do you think?'

The strange voice spoke. 'I believe so. It's pretty clear.'

Mum lifted the toddler up and balanced her on her hip. 'Can you say bye-bye, Cassie?'

The little girl waved. 'Auf Wiedersehen.'

'No, Cassie, say *bye-bye*.'

Confused, the little girl hid her face. Mum looked stricken then headed for the kitchen swaying with the extra weight. As they left a small voice said, 'Ich liebe dich, Mama.'

There was silence for a moment as the video continued to record the room in their absence. Dad glanced at the faceless woman behind the camera. 'Are you certain it's German?'

'Quite certain.'

'Alright.' He visibly gathered himself. 'That was my daughter,

Cassie. My wife and I don't speak German, although we've picked up a few words now . . . We didn't teach her this.' He ran his hands through his hair again. 'It started when she began to talk five months ago. She . . . she won't speak any English, other than names like Bunny. We don't know what this means, but we're recording this because one day we might need to prove that this happened . . . It might mean something . . . W-we hope it doesn't.'

The video whirred on for a moment, immortalising his anxiety, then the picture quivered and turned to static.

My hands had fallen to my lap. I clasped them together until they ached and stared at my parents. They still looked at the screen as if the ghosts of their younger selves were imprinted on the glass.

I felt as if I was on a fairground waltzer. Implications of what I had seen whirled around me and my head pounded. There had to be a rational explanation. Desperately I clutched at the one idea that had occurred while I was watching the film. 'I-I'm adopted?' Even I could hear the pitiful hopefulness in my voice.

Mum blinked. 'Oh, Cassie,' she said. 'No, that's not right at all.' She glared at Dad. 'I told you we should have explained things to her first.'

Dad slumped further into the low armchair. He made no move to switch off the television and the hiss of static continued in front of us as if something was trying to break into the room. 'You think you're adopted? You think that's what that shows?'

I bit my lip. 'If that little girl is me . . . then she's not English.'

Mum moved her hand to hover over mine, but didn't let it fall. 'That was you, Cassie, and you're ours.' She flexed her fingers. 'I mean you aren't adopted. I can fetch your birth certificate if you want.'

'Then how do you explain this?' I gestured at the television in sudden anger.

Dad leaned forward and his face was inscrutable. 'You spoke German before you spoke English. You had whole sentences in German before you could even say "bye-bye".'

'That doesn't make sense.' I swallowed. I needed to think about this. 'Who was the woman recording the video? Why did you say your name was Dave Smith? What house was that? It had our things in it.'

Dad glanced at Mum and groaned. 'Alright . . . when you were about twenty months your language was quite a long way behind your friends. We were worried so we took you to see the health visitor.' His Adam's apple bobbed. 'Her father was Swiss so she realised straight away that you were talking German. Eventually she helped us find a doctor. Doctor Ashworth: a specialist in past lives.'

'P-past lives,' I spluttered. 'You're kidding me.'

Dad flushed: 'We were desperate; we didn't know what was going on and the Doctor seemed so rational when we called her.'

Mum knotted her hand into her skirt. 'You won't remember her, honey. You spent a lot of time with her when you were little, but she started acting like she owned you . . .'

'We told her we didn't want you to see her any more, but she wouldn't leave us alone.' Dad clenched his fists. 'She kept badgering us to send you to some special school where she could monitor you twenty-four hours a day. She interfered all the time and never took no for an answer.' The lines on his face deepened and his mouth turned down. 'Then you started having the nightmares.'

Mum flinched and her face twisted. 'We just wanted you to live a normal life, not be some sort of . . . science experiment. One day the Doctor turned up with all this equipment and tried to get into the house. I told her you were napping and made an appointment to go to her office instead.'

Dad reached out as if he wanted to pat Mum's hand, but the distance between his chair and the sofa was too great. 'We realised we'd made a mistake letting her into your life. So we went to stay with your nan and put the house on the market. Your mum gave up her job. We even changed our name.'

'Changed our name?' I looked around the room as if I was seeing it for the first time.

'That's right.' Dad cleared this throat. 'You were born Cassiopeia Mae Smith.'

I inhaled, too stunned to react further. 'I-I thought I was born in this house.'

Mum pulled my hand to her lap. 'The Doctor was convinced you were having past-life memories, Cassie. Your dad and I, we've been racking our brains for years and we can't think of anything else this could be. There's no other explanation that isn't even more far-fetched. When we moved down here and you started nursery you stopped speaking German, like you forgot it. But you never grew out of the nightmares and at school German was so easy for you, as if you were remembering instead of learning.

Your dad didn't think you should carry on with the lessons. He thought it might make the nightmares worse.' She hesitated and I stared at him.

'Why didn't you tell me? I thought . . .'

'I know.' Dad refused to catch my eye. 'But we didn't think we were ever going to tell you this. It was better that you thought I was being unreasonable.'

Over my stunned silence Mum continued to talk. 'I got you that book, *Learn Lucid Dreaming*, because it was by Doctor Ashworth. I thought it might help.'

I shook my head and Dad exhaled. 'Now there's this thing with Hopfingen. *Was* it you who left the anonymous tip they were talking about?'

I winced, unable to answer.

'We'll not mention that again.' He dropped his head into his hands. 'I-I don't know what to do, Marie.' He spoke into his palms, but his eyes went to the card on top of the video box. 'Do we use the number?'

Mum's grip tightened on my arm. 'It should be up to Cassie.' She looked at me. 'The Doctor might be able to tell us more about this. She might even be able to help, but then again . . .'

I tightened my hands on hers. 'I could end up as some sort of science experiment.'

Mum said nothing, but Dad's fists closed round handfuls of his hair.

'I need some time to think about this.'

Mum nodded. 'Take all the time you need.'

'I should go to school.'

'School?'

'I need to think about something else for a few hours, get some perspective.'

'Alright, love. I'll let them know you'll be coming in after all. Your dad'll drive you.'

I slouched into history part way through the third period. The class was gathered around a table, notebooks in hand.

'Cassie, good of you to join us. Feeling better?'

I nodded and Mr Greene pointed to the table. 'Find a spot.'

I edged my way between my classmates then angled myself so I could see the table. It was covered in newspapers. Some of the papers were national: broadsheets and tabloids, but others looked like local German papers.

'Cassie, I'll recap for your benefit. We have a fantastic chance to explore history in action. You might have heard the news this morning.' The blood pounded in my ears and I gripped the table edge.

Why didn't I expect this?

Mr Greene was giddy with enthusiasm. His skinny wrists poked out of his jacket as he waved his arms over the print on the table. 'I want us to look at the differences in how this event is being reported at an international, a national and a local level. I want essays on how the local press is reacting, and on any differences between the ways the Germans and English are seeing this. You should all be able to produce some *fantastic* coursework. The exam board is going to be very impressed. We were almost on the spot, as it were.'

He flicked a copy of the *Daily Telegraph*. 'I want your essays backed up by historical fact. You can use information from our visits to Flossenbürg and Bayreuth and go to the library – I don't want information from dodgy websites. Please provide proper bibliographies.' He raised his hands. 'Here is a selection of papers. This all actually happened a few days ago, so the local ones are older than the nationals. Get started.'

My classmates descended like wasps round a Coke can, excited about the turn of events. When the table had cleared and I was no longer being jostled, all that was left was a single copy of a three-day-old community paper, written in German.

Mr Greene looked at me with something like sympathy and his moustache twitched. 'Start with that one, Cassie. If you have trouble with the translation, speak to Miss Barnes.'

I swallowed and, left with no choice, reached for the smudged paper. I used one finger to turn it round.

On the front page there was a picture I recognised: a young, tensely smiling Karla Ehrlichmann standing in front of her sweet shop. The headline did not focus on the grisly find in the field. Instead it read Selbsmord in Hopfingen.

It took me a moment to translate the line then I had to hold the table with both hands to keep my knees from buckling. Astrid's great-aunt Karla, who in my memories lived young and candy-scented and who harboured a fondness for a long-dead boy, had killed herself.

I read on, translating unconsciously. The old lady had left a suicide note in which she wrote about the Jewish exodus from

Hopfingen. She said the families had been made to gather outside her own sweetshop and that she couldn't live with the fact that they had been taken to their deaths and she had done nothing.

In my mind I saw her hand a bag of sweets to Zillah. *'You'll be with your own kind. It'll be good for everyone, you'll see.'*

I *had* been wrong to call the police.

My hands shook as I made the decision to call Doctor Ashworth, ignoring the most important lesson of Karla's death: the past should remain buried.

CHAPTER FIVE

THE DOCTOR

Mum and I perched on a red sofa in the Doctor's reception area. Our knees nudged a table laid with magazines like *Eve*, *Livingetc* and an incongruous, dog-eared *Beano*. Neither of us picked anything up.

A slim blonde was sitting behind the desk and murmuring into a telephone. Her beige dress was almost the same colour as the walls; a red brooch was the only spot of colour in her outfit.

Mum leaned close. Her breath smelled of the single gin Dad had pressed on her earlier. 'Do you think she's colour coordinated on purpose?'

I snorted and the receptionist twisted away from us to continue her call.

Mum checked her watch with a frown. Then she patted my knee, rose and went to the desk, her shoes clattering a staccato on the light wood floor. 'Excuse me?'

The blonde raised one finger and carried on with her conversation.

Mum leaned forward. 'My daughter, Cassie Farrier, has a three o'clock appointment and I don't want the Doctor to think we're late.'

The receptionist tossed her hair as though desperately inconvenienced. One finger tapped a rhythm on her mouse as she looked at the computer screen, then she narrowed her eyes at Mum as if measuring the woman in front of her against the details on her display. Finally, she laid the receiver down and pressed a button beneath her desk. 'Doctor Ashworth, your three o'clock is here.'

Instantly I forgot her rudeness. My toes tingled and I screwed them up inside my shoes as I lurched to my feet. I was about to reverse my parents' decision to flee from the Doctor all those years ago.

What if she's angry?

The receptionist gestured towards the frosted glass door guarded by her desk. 'The Doctor is on her way.'

Mum pulled me to her side and we stood, eyes pinned to the entrance, like gladiators awaiting our opponent. Then, with a slight hiss, the door opened and I saw the Doctor for the first time.

My eyes widened and I couldn't suppress a gasp; she was huge, a billboard image torn out and brought to life. Her legs were like a wrestler's and her hands would have swamped Dad's, yet she wore a designer suit and moved like a dancer.

Mum's fingers pressed mine as the Doctor bent over the receptionist's keyboard.

'She hasn't aged a single day.' Mum paused in the act of reaching for her own face and lowered her voice almost to a breath. 'Don't mention the video, alright?' I glanced at her bag, where I knew the tape nestled next to her wallet and keys. 'If she doesn't remember us, I don't want to remind her who we are. Not unless I have to.'

I nodded, abruptly cold in the air-conditioned space, and my eyes slid back to the Doctor. 'She's so *big*.'

Mum nodded wordlessly and squeezed my hand tighter.

At that moment the Doctor turned from the receptionist and her eyes lingered on me. A cold hard core glittered in their depths like the death of a star. I stepped backwards, she blinked and abruptly they were ordinary blue eyes, bright with curious intelligence.

'Cassie Farrier?'

Mum nodded and tugged on my wrist as the Doctor reopened the door and held it for us.

'Follow me,' she said.

The corridor connected four doors. The Doctor paused before the last and waited for us to reach her. Relative to her size, the portal seemed oddly small, like a gateway to Wonderland, and I shivered as she gestured us through.

Inside, however, we found only a sparsely furnished office. In the centre of the room was an oriental rug and on the rug, a large, old-fashioned desk. The desk itself was empty apart from a silver laptop customised with the Orion's Belt logo that had also decorated the entrance to the building.

Two chairs waited for us. As we sat down, the door closed behind us with a quiet click.

The Doctor lowered herself into a leather seat and I fidgeted uncomfortably until she spoke. 'Tell me your problem.'

Immediately Mum's right hand groped for mine. Tension thrummed through her fingers and she held on so tightly I could feel the pulse in her thumb. 'It's about my daughter.' Mum cleared her throat. 'We hope you'll be able to help her.'

The Doctor spoke slowly. 'Are you aware that I'm a specialist?'

A tremor entered Mum's voice. 'Yes. Y-you're interested in past lives.'

'And your daughter thinks she has lived a past life?' The Doctor's nose wrinkled and she looked at me as if I was a germ on a Petri dish. Then she turned back to Mum. 'I do a lot of research in that area and it is very rare to come across genuine past-life memories. Most people I see are charlatans, or are suffering from very ordinary nightmares or in some cases are recounting details from old television series in which they have recast themselves.' She leaned forward; her size alone was threatening. 'I must tell you, Mrs Farrier, that if you and your daughter are trying to con me, I will find out.' She swivelled her torso to include me in her warning and Mum jumped to her feet, still holding my hand.

The Doctor leaned back, her behaviour no longer so intimidating, but Mum remained standing. 'We're here because we need help. Cassie's nightmares are out of control. She barely gets any rest. Sleeping tablets don't help.'

'Is that so?' The Doctor's flawless lips curved into a conciliatory smile and she waved Mum back down.

Mum swallowed as she subsided. 'Th-that's not all.'

'Not all?' The Doctor's thin brows raised.

'Have you heard the news about the mass grave discovered in Germany?'

The Doctor inclined her head.

Surprised, I tugged at Mum's hand. Dad had told us not to mention that to anyone. Mum ignored me. 'The anonymous tip that led police to the site was left by my daughter.'

I watched the Doctor to see how she took the news, and at first it seemed she hadn't even heard. Then she turned and addressed me for the first time. 'Are you lying?'

I shook my head.

'Trying to get attention, perhaps? Many children your age feel undervalued at home. Do you want to be famous?' she mused.

I glared. 'I can tell you the exact message the anonymous caller left and I can tell you the phone box the call was made from. Is there a way to check that information with the police?'

She nodded. 'There is.' She typed briefly. 'We'll discuss those details at the end of the session. For now I want you to tell me what made you leave that message.'

Her eyes burned hungrily. There was something about this Doctor that made my heart beat like prey.

'I'm waiting, Miss Farrier,' she snapped.

I blew out a breath and ignored my discomfort. The Doctor scared me but I needed her help . . . so I told her everything as clearly as I could.

When I finished speaking the Doctor's eyes flicked to the microphone on the side of her laptop and it struck me that she'd recorded the whole conversation. She remained that way, staring at the computer, as the clock above her head ticked away the seconds and seemed to grow louder and louder. Then she looked at my mother. 'You believe your daughter?'

Mum nodded.

'Hmmm.' The Doctor picked up a pencil and rolled it between her fingertips. 'Well, Mrs Farrier, I would like you and your daughter to read my book and use the techniques for three weeks. If there's no improvement, I'll see you again.' She conjured a copy of *Learn Lucid Dreaming* from her desk and pushed it across the leather blotter.

Instantly I leaped to my feet. I glowered at Mum. 'I should

have known she wouldn't be able to help when you told me she wrote that thing.'

'Cassie!'

The Doctor focused on me. 'You know this text?'

'It's *rubbish*.'

She pressed her hands together, apparently unoffended. 'Did you use it properly?'

I hammered my fists on the desk, so angry I almost spat. The hope that had started to warm my chest drained and left me cold. 'It didn't work.'

Mum took my hand and pulled me back. 'Come on, Cassie, we'll go somewhere else.'

'Hold on.' The book disappeared. 'I wrote that book because so many of my patients come to me suffering from bad dreams inspired by half-remembered historical fiction. I've become an expert on dreaming and the techniques in the book *do* work.'

I started to deny it but she lifted one plate-like palm and I stuttered into silence.

'The techniques work for people who are suffering from simple nightmares. If you'd used the book properly your bad dreams should have been relieved. Ninety-nine times out of a hundred I send a patient away with that book and they never have to come back.' Again the tight smile. 'You say you've used the book already? Are you certain you followed the instructions?'

I glared. 'Are you saying you don't believe me?' The Doctor patted the air condescendingly and I spun to face Mum. 'Show her the video.'

Mum's hands covered her bag protectively. 'I don't think *that's* necessary.' Her eyes flickered and I clenched my fists.

'We've already told her about Germany and she still isn't taking us seriously. She won't help me unless she believes us. Show her the video.'

'Video?' The Doctor's eyebrows twitched.

Slowly, Mum pulled out the tape. She hesitated, fingers tightening on the cassette. Then she placed it on the desk with a snap.

The Doctor pressed a button on the side of her desk. 'Sandra, I need the old VCR.'

We watched the video together, the Doctor with a frightening intensity. She took no notes, but I got the feeling that she'd forget nothing on the screen. Once she looked at Mum but her expression was of carefully schooled blankness and I couldn't tell what she was thinking before she turned away.

She remembered us now. I wondered what she would say when the video ended.

When the static returned I fidgeted, as if I was to blame for the fact that Mum and Dad had removed me from the Doctor's influence, but all she said was, 'Interesting.'

Mum slumped. 'I'm sure you have something you want to say to me.'

The Doctor pursed her lips and I held my breath.

Then she shook her head. 'I don't think so, Mrs *Farrier*. This *reminder* has shown me your daughter is, in all probability, suffering from genuine past-life memories. I still believe I can help her. As you've returned to my offices I assume that you are now willing to allow me to do so?'

My thumbs pricked and as Mum nodded I rubbed my hands on my jeans.

She could have sent us away or at least made this much harder for Mum. Why didn't she?

The Doctor looked at me and her lips twisted into a smile that made my stomach lurch. 'Let's get started.'

CHAPTER SIX

THERAPY

I was lying on a bed. It would have been comfortable, but I was covered in plastic tabs that led to humming monitors and my head was shut inside a metal helmet.

Mum forced a smile, but I could read her thoughts as if they were branded on her forehead: *I had become a science experiment.*

The Doctor was checking monitors and rolls of paper. She moved around me like a lion nearing a gazelle: she pretended to be interested in other things, yet every time she glanced my way I sensed her keen awareness.

Mum leaned into me. 'It isn't too late, Cassie. We don't have to do this.'

Although the Doctor acted as if she hadn't heard, her movements sharpened and my heart hammered.

Briefly I closed my eyes. 'We do have to do this,' I muttered.

'Alright then. I'll be right here.'

The Doctor dropped one huge hand on to Mum's shoulder and she jumped like a toddler caught with a marker pen. 'Actually,

Mrs *Farrier* . . . or is it Mrs Smith?' The Doctor tilted her head. Her tone was blandly polite, but I frowned.

Mum licked her lips. 'It's Mrs Farrier now.'

'Mrs Farrier then. Actually I'm going to have to ask you to step outside.'

'Mum?' I knew I sounded pathetic but I didn't want to be left alone.

The Doctor moved to stand over me. I strained to sit up so I wouldn't feel so helpless, but the wires and helmet held me down.

'We can't have your mother in here because her presence might affect the readings.' The Doctor placed her hand just beneath my breast bone. She wasn't applying any pressure, but through her palm I received a clear idea of her weight and strength and I froze. 'Even I won't be in here with you. We'll both be observing from right over there.' With her free hand she indicated a large mirror on the wall and I realised it must be two-way. I shivered.

'Are you cold? The temperature in here is constant, so you shouldn't be. Don't forget, when you wake up, the first thing you need to do is recount your dream. Speak out loud the first words that come into your head. Don't think, just start talking. I'll be recording everything.'

My bare feet curled. 'I won't fall asleep in here.'

The Doctor picked up a syringe. 'Yes, you will.'

The sedative drowned my flutters of panic like flies in jam. I left behind the fear with which I usually faced unconsciousness and, as the drug pulled me into the darkness, was able to wonder hazily whether Zillah would come to me immediately or if I would have a new vision.

It began with a book.

With the odd detachment you get in dreams I noted that the one time I needed to relive the horrors of my past life, I was going to get a nightmare that couldn't possibly relate. The irony was a mild nagging that died alongside my urge to waken.

The book was lurking at the end of a long tunnel. Although I couldn't see it clearly I knew the binding was scaled like the hide of a long-dead beast. Slowly it opened and dread deadened my spine as I was pulled towards its pages.

I struggled to remain as far away as possible, but the current was relentless, and as I was sucked forward the tunnel around me filled with numberless others, all fighting just as fruitlessly for escape.

Faces familiar from my nightmare tumbled past: Zillah cried out with a childish wail. Then the Nazi who had shot her howled and reached for me as though I could save him.

Other characters felt like they were from stories I'd once read. There was another soldier, American this time, whose insignia flashed in the strange half light to reveal the words *27th Division*. He was followed by a terrifying apparition in a white pointed hood. Then I saw a cowled inquisitor, a cleric, one of Cromwell's followers, a Roman mercenary and an Egyptian priest. There were dozens more that I didn't recognise and they blurred past me in a dizzying vortex as the book sucked them in.

Finally it was my turn. But before I slammed into the hungry maw, I glimpsed one final figure: a long-haired youth whose mismatched light and dark brown eyes were warm with a blend of curiosity and desire.

With a slight frown the boy reached for my hand, almost as if he recognised me, but before our palms could kiss, he was drawn into the pages like a flower pressed into an album.

Searing pain almost stopped my heart then I too was inside.

I gasped and the scene dissolved . . .

* * *

I hurl my jammed weapon aside as I run; it's only dead weight now and slowing me down.

My breath comes in bursts, blade-sharp, and I know I have to stop soon. But as the idea slides in I push onwards: I'm the only one left alive. If I stop, they'll find me and I won't survive the interrogation.

Suddenly my feet slip. I throw my arms out, but there is no ground to catch my fall. I pitch down a hill and howl as barbed wire wraps me like the arms of a Nixe.

For one moment I hang suspended from the fence, a deformed scarecrow. There the rain washes my face and I catch my breath, trying to gauge how badly I'm cut.

Too late I hear a creak. I start to wriggle but, before I can escape, the posts give way – and this time when I fall barbed wire is tangled around me.

Every time I hit the hillside it's agony. The thud and crash of plummeting fence posts surrounds me and I try to cover my head as I come to rest at the bottom of the slope.

Foolishly I roll and my movement tugs at the last post standing. The rain disguises the crack of rotting timber, but then the final stake hammers into my thighs and drives quills of wire through my trousers.

I scream and curse; my uniform is as much protection as soggy paper. Every breath forces metal thorns into my skin and I can't move without unbelievable pain.

Whimpering I strain to pierce the curtain of rain. I can see nothing but swampland, empty of life. I hitch a breath and raise my head, looking for help. Seeing no one, I let my cheek fall into a hollow.

For a moment exhaustion overtakes me. I can't remember the last time I slept in a bed and, even then, nightmares drove me awake. A trancelike state brings relief that's almost pleasant. I allow myself to drift, not quite conscious.

But then the hollow fills with water, I have to lift my head and the twin torments of pain and panic return.

Someone must have been tracking me. They had to have seen me fall.

Volleys of rain drench my back. Chilled, I groan through chattering teeth. Even that small movement works the barbs further in.

My blood fouls the puddle as it creeps up my cheek. I turn one eye to face the lashing rain. The horizon is grey. No sunlight spears the earth; no blue breaks the cloud. It looks like the end of the world.

With every other breath now I have to clear my mouth. My neck cramps as I try to hold my head out of the deepening quagmire and, although I wouldn't have thought it possible, the cramp hurts as much as the barbed wire does.

I try to squirm free of the wood that pins me. I only have to move a few inches to escape the water but I can't. The wire and my cramping muscles keep me frozen in place. For the first time in my life I cannot make my body obey me.

The rain pounds on. It is as though God himself intends to hold my face in the water. I let my neck droop, but when my lungs set on fire I pull it up again.

My neck seizes and a spasm crackles along my back. Wire tears my skin. Too weak even to scream, I cry for the woman I love and let my head fall; I cannot lift it again.

And yet at the end, I am almost relieved. Now there will be no more nightmares.

'Help me.'

'Describe the dream – don't let it go.'

'Somebody help!' It must have been the drugs but I was in a strange half-and-half place. I knew I was awake, but was so filled with the dream that I was drowned in the terror of it.

I struggled against the wires that held me down and cracked my head on the metal helmet. I screamed for help and although I barely knew what I was saying I was unable to resist the Doctor's instructions.

'Gun's jammed. Blood in my eyes. Can't see. They're after me. Killed the others. Falling into barbed wire. Wraps like a Nixe.' I screamed as pains sizzled once more along my arms and legs. Distantly I registered the hoarseness of my own voice. 'Post landed on me. Can't move. Help me.'

Mum's arms enveloped me. 'Cassie, I'm here, it's alright.'

'Mrs Farrier, you're ruining my readings. You need to step away.'

'You have enough. Get my daughter out of this thing.'

'What's a *Nixe*?'

'What?'

I was huddled in a chair back in the Doctor's office. A blanket was wrapped around my shoulders but my teeth still chattered and my thighs twitched with phantom pains. This new dream had been the worst by far and my shaking wasn't only due to the memory of unutterable cold.

'A *Nixe*, what is it?'

'I d-don't know. I've never heard that word before.' Something tickled the back of my head, a thought like a feather, but I couldn't grasp it.

'You said it when you woke up; you must know what it means.' The Doctor didn't seem worried or annoyed. She typed a note on her computer and looked at me, quizzical.

'I really d-don't.' I shook my head and clutched the blanket tighter.

'Interesting.' The Doctor met my gaze and in her eyes I saw an abyss. Disorientated, I rocked in my chair as she turned to my mother and cut me out of the conversation. 'Mrs Farrier, we need to run more tests.' She held up a palm as Mum's back stiffened. 'I don't want to get too technical, but the equipment showed that when Cassie was asleep it wasn't just her brainstem, the part of her brain that normally deals with sleep, that was active. It was her whole brain, particularly the amygdalae, which deal with what's called emotional memory.'

Mum shuffled her feet.

Good . . . Mum doesn't understand either.

The Doctor sighed. 'Basically, Mrs Smith, your daughter wasn't just dreaming, she was remembering.'

Mum pursed her lips. 'How can she remember something that hasn't happened to her?'

Mum's right – that's impossible.

The Doctor steepled her fingers. 'The event did happen to her, but not in this lifetime.'

Mum frowned. 'But the dream she just had, it's different from the one that she's been having about the little girl.' She looked at me for confirmation and I nodded.

The Doctor regarded me as if I was an autopsied frog. 'Do you have a number of different, violent dreams?'

I thought of the recent variations in my night-time horror show. This was the first time the Doctor had said anything that sounded as if she truly understood what was happening to me and I nodded eagerly.

The Doctor hummed and turned to Mum once more. 'If your daughter has been reincarnated, there's no reason to assume it has only happened once. Her strongest memories will be from the most recent lifetime and, strengthened even more by the physical stimuli of her visit to Germany, they may have led her to the gravesite.' She tapped her nails on the desk and went on. 'However, she could also be experiencing memories from earlier incarnations and there may be any number of them. From the description she gave us, the dream-memory she experienced today could have been from any historically recent conflict, the First World War for example.'

Mum nodded but I struggled for breath.

I'll never be cured.

I hunched further into the chair as the weight of a hundred lives pressed down on me. The image of the little Jewish girl floated in front of my eyes.

If the Doctor manages to get rid of Zillah another ghost will be there to take her place.

Hopelessly I opened my eyes to find the Doctor still speaking.

'When your daughter first woke up she may have been speaking partially as an earlier personality. She was using words that her conscious self doesn't know. I had Sandra do some research.' The Doctor consulted her notes. 'A *Nixe* was a water spirit that caused the drowning and miserable death of many German men.' She smiled faintly. 'It seems your daughter's previous self was rather superstitious.'

Mum's grip tightened. 'Can you help her?'

The Doctor's lips twitched. 'This would have been easier if she had been younger, but we can use hypnosis to bring her most recent previous self forward. Then there's a technique called Rolfing, in which we stimulate certain muscles to reactivate repressed memories and help emotions to the surface.'

I pulled my hand from Mum's and jumped to my feet. 'Wait a minute! I don't want to remember this stuff more clearly. You're supposed to be finding a way to get rid of my nightmares.'

The Doctor cocked her head at me. 'You need to experience these repressed emotions on a conscious level so you can learn to deal with them on every level: waking and sleeping.'

As if my legs had been cut out from under me I sagged back into the chair.

The Doctor removed a glossy brochure from her desk drawer and addressed Mum. 'Look at this and get back to me, Mrs Farrier. We can talk about a financial plan later, if it's an issue, but if I'm really to help, I need your daughter *here*.' A manicured nail brushed the front of the leaflet.

I craned my neck as mum turned the brochure over. It looked like a country house. 'I-is this is where you wanted to take her thirteen years ago?'

The tip of a very pink tongue appeared between the Doctor's

lips. 'It's a facility where I work with a small team on *real* cases of reincarnation. If you decide you want my help, your daughter would have to move in. She would receive the best physiological and psychiatric care, all the techniques we talked about.' She glanced at me. 'We also have a pool and tennis court for leisure time.'

Absently Mum gave her stock answer. 'Cassie doesn't like the water.'

I leaned over her arm for a better view of the brochure. 'How long would I have to stay?'

'Until we agree you've made progress.' The Doctor shrugged. 'Normally a few *months*.'

'A few months.' Mum's head shot up. 'What about school?'

The Doctor shrugged. 'I can see you have a lot to think about. Don't hesitate to call the office once you've made your decision.'

Our appointment was over.

PART THREE

INCARCERATION

'Heaven shall remain closed to you . . . Unless the spirits you created in your lust overcome the restrictions of their fleshly bodies you will remain in this prison until the end of the world.'

CHAPTER SEVEN

MOUNT HERMON

Something had come loose. It had been rattling in the boot for the last ten miles. Dad twitched every time it knocked into my case but he didn't stop to fix it.

'It's raining again,' Mum murmured.

It had been a nice day when we'd set off but sporadic showers had begun just beyond Leeds: they changed lumbering lorries into terrifying beasts and painted the world grey.

Now off the motorway the colours changed and all around us rambling dry-stone walls cut across moors that glowed silver and mauve through the sheets of rain. It almost looked as if we were driving underwater.

Despite the jolting of the pock-marked roads I held my forehead to the window. I should have been feeling anticipation or excitement, but instead my stomach rolled with a jumble of travel sickness and queasy dread.

After a while I rubbed the tops of my shoulders and wondered if I could face Mum's concern if I asked for a Nurofen.

Dad glanced at Mum. 'Have you got the map?' It was the first time he'd spoken since we'd left the motorway.

Mum unfolded a piece of A4 paper from her handbag and a lump settled in my throat.

We must be nearly there.

Mum obviously thought so too, because she turned in her seat. 'You'll behave, won't you?'

I nodded.

Dad grunted. 'Don't think this is some sort of holiday. You'll work to get well and when you come home you'll study. Seeing as you won't be able to do your exams this year, I expect your grades next year to be massively improved.'

I thought about the part-time work I'd just given up. 'I'll help pay for this. I can get another job.'

Dad jerked and Mum twisted aginst her seatbelt. 'You'll do no such thing.' Her shoulders dropped. 'Pumpkin, if you want to get a part-time job when you get home, that's up to you. We want you to enjoy feeling healthy and happy, and if getting a job is part of it, that's okay, but the money you earn, you keep. Dad and I are paying for this.'

Dad nodded.

'But . . .'

'Enough, Cassiopeia. We'll manage.' Dad slowed the car. 'What turn am I looking for?'

Mum looked at the paper in her hand. 'We're coming up to a village called Harmon and looking for a left turning by the post office.'

Sure enough, as we turned a corner, a village appeared as if dropped there by the mist that coiled over the streams.

Over the village green a pub sign creaked loud enough to hear over the engine. It read *The Blacksmith's Arms*. The crimson Post Office sign glowed next to it and an old-fashioned red telephone box guarded the other side of the road.

'There.' Mum pointed to a half-hidden junction and Dad turned the wheel.

The houses quickly thinned until only occasional outlying properties were left. They clung to the village boundary like remote stars in an expanding universe.

As we passed the final house, chickens reacted to the sound of our car and lined up the garden wall like a militia. The house had once been painted white but giant peeling patches and brown mottling gave the appearance of diseased neglect. With no little sense of irony I read the crooked sign pinned to the gatepost: Hope Farm.

Mum's knees began to jump up and down uncontrollably.

'Mum?'

She started to speak as if I hadn't. 'You have to work to get well, Cassie. If this fails . . .' She balled her fists on her knees. 'Doctor Ashworth thinks she can help you, so you have to let her try.' I met her eyes in the mirror. They were as wet as the car window. 'This is all we've got,' she whispered.

I didn't know if she meant that the Doctor held all our hopes or all our money and I didn't ask, because it didn't matter either way.

If the Doctor can't help me, I'll have to stay this way for the rest of my life.

Suddenly the car crunched on gravel and Dad slowed. Whatever was rattling in the boot crashed into the suitcase and stopped.

There was a sign in front of us: Mount Hermon. Beneath the name was the Orion's Belt logo I'd last seen on the Doctor's laptop; it was the colour of blood. There was no building and no gate, just the sign and a long gravel drive. We speeded up again.

Finally we rounded a corner and I had my first view of Mount Hermon. It was bigger than it had seemed on the brochure and I gasped; it looked like the set of an old film.

The wide steps glistened with recent rainfall but, as I watched, the sun eased through the clouds and gleamed on the cream stone. A shaft of light glinted from a window pane and drew my attention to a set of bars.

Why are there bars on the windows?

With a final rattle and crunch the car rolled to a halt and Dad heaved on the handbrake. Not one of us moved.

Then a sharp crack just by my head made me jump and my door was opened from the outside.

Nostrils flaring, my head snapped up. A boy leaned on the roof-rack, long hair shifting in the breeze. Recognition whipped the air from my lungs. The boy had, quite literally, stepped out of a nightmare . . . the one from the Doctor's office.

My heart started to race.

Frantically I searched my memory; maybe we'd met somewhere. His hair was neater than I remembered and tied into a ponytail at the base of his neck. The style revealed the presence of a twisting scar that snaked from beneath his right ear lobe to the collar of his shirt. It made him look . . . dangerous.

Our gazes met and the boy's own intake of breath was obvious.

Could I be as familiar to him as he is to me?

His eyes widened as I continued to stare. The left was the colour of melted chocolate, the right, while still brown, was so light it was almost gold. I blinked, slightly confused by the odd sense that there were two people in there.

Then I noticed how deeply his eyes were sunk, as though bruising from a heavy beating was only just fading. More specifically as though he'd never enjoyed a good night's sleep.

Whoever he is . . . this boy is like me.

The boy's eyes flicked to my parents but he spoke to me. 'Are you going to sit there all day?'

Embarrassed into movement, I unlocked my seatbelt and slid towards the door. 'We've come all this way . . . I might as well get out of the car.'

But my legs had cramped after hours in one position. When I winced the boy offered me a hand. Automatically I wrapped my fingers round his. One of the boy's knuckles was swollen. Thoughtlessly I ran the pad of my thumb over the old injury.

He cleared his throat and flushing hotly I leaped from the car and pulled my hand free.

What am I doing?

Dad stood next to me and held out his palm. 'Dave Farrier.'

They shook hands. 'Seth Alexander.'

Dad nodded. 'This is my daughter, Cassie, and my wife, Marie.'

'Hi.' Seth turned to me.

'H-hi.'

My thoughts stuttered. Seth looked like a hero from an old story. Nicola would have called him 'well fit' but he was more than that. He was beautiful. Immediately I clamped down on the thought as if he could read my mind.

'I've been sent to help with your bags and show you to your room.'

With an uncharacteristic show of heartiness, Dad patted my back and went to open the boot.

I had a wheeled case and a smaller bag. Dad took the case and Seth hefted the bag on to his shoulder. His shirt strained across his back and I exhaled. I tried to look away, but my gaze shifted to the fit of his jeans. For something to do I sank my hands into my hair and tightened my ponytail. Mum caught my elbow as Dad and Seth crunched towards the steps.

'You're here to get better.' Her voice was exasperated.

'I know.'

Why did she have to see me looking at him?

'You need to focus on your health, not on boys.'

I dug my toes into wet gravel. *'I know.'*

Mum touched my chin. 'I know you know, pumpkin, but please be careful. That lad is older than you. You haven't had much experience with this sort of thing and now isn't the time. When you're well you'll meet someone.'

I ducked away. 'He's hardly spoken to me, Mum. And he wouldn't be interested anyway.' Angrily I gestured, taking in my cheap clothes, lazy hair and pallid complexion.

Mum shook her head again, slowly, and her mouth turned down. 'I don't want you to get hurt.'

I moved to follow Dad. 'No one's going to get hurt.'

Mum was one step behind me as I stomped up the stairs.

If Mum had spotted me looking at Seth, he might have noticed too.

Humiliation carried me straight through the large double doors.

Inside, I stopped and my mouth fell open. Seth and Dad were ahead; they waited on the carpet at the top of a sweeping staircase that peeled off in two directions. The carpet was the colour of weeds, the wood something dark . . . mahogany maybe. The light that spilled in from the windows, already rain-washed, was absorbed into the pile and gave the place a murky look, as if we stood in a cavern.

On the ground floor the carpet arced around the staircase and disappeared into dark glass doors to both left and right. Embossed plaques hung over each entrance. To my right the brass was etched with *Dining, Leisure, Classrooms*. To my left it simply said *Treatment Area*.

Seth waved his free hand. 'I'll give you the tour later.'

My trainers whispered on the stairs and I trailed my fingertips along the banister as I climbed. The wood was smooth and unmarked. My hand twitched with the sudden urge to find some way of making an impression on the indifferent wood and stone. Suddenly dizzy I blinked and had to shake my head to clear it.

Seth twisted to the left and his scar stood out over his skin like a wire. 'Boys' accommodation.' He nodded right as Mum stretched to see past him. 'Girls'. We each have our own room.' He glanced at the bags under my eyes. 'I guess you know why the rooms here aren't shared.'

I nodded and a small weight lifted from my chest. I'd been wondering if I'd have a roommate. For some reason I'd pictured Mount Hermon as an old-fashioned boarding school, with ranks of bunk beds lined against a wall.

Seth opened the door on his right. The corridor curved ahead and I inhaled. 'How many rooms *are* there?'

Seth cocked his head. 'Do you mean how many patients?' I nodded and he shifted the weight of my bag. 'These rooms aren't all full. With you, there are eight of us: four girls, four boys. I'm the oldest, Lenny's ten.'

'That's so young.' I tried to imagine what it would be like to be ten and in this place, but a girl's shriek interrupted me.

'Kyle!'

A door slammed, Seth grunted and I threw myself against the wall as a slim boy bounded round the corner. He looked like a miniature rocker, with spiked black hair, skinny black jeans and big boots. A grin split his lips and, although they were deep set, his eyes were a brighter green than the carpet.

He wielded a camera phone in one hand as he skidded to a halt next to Seth. 'My man!'

Seth shook himself and glanced at my parents. 'What're you doing, Kyle?'

'Double Dares.' He tucked the phone into his jeans.

'Not Lizzie's stupid game . . . where is she?'

'Where d'you think she is? Doing the boys' side.'

Seth frowned towards the boys' accommodation and, I assumed, his own room. He opened his mouth, but just then a girl pounded after Kyle. 'Get back here, you gargoyle. When I've torn off your arms I'm gonna smash that phone with the stumps.'

'Gotta go, man.' Kyle ducked past Dad and hit the doors running.

When the girl saw us she dug the toes of her boots into the carpet to bring herself to a halt. She was bright red and shaking. Even the tips of her ears, rimmed with silver studs, were glowing. 'I'm not finished with you,' she shouted as Kyle leaped down the stairs.

Moving closer to my parents I stared unashamedly. The girl was worth looking at.

Her eyes were the colour of faded denim and lined with thick kohl. Peroxide-white hair was cut pixie short and spiked around her ears and forehead. It framed the studs that marched up her lobes and the single bar that bisected her eyebrow. She wasn't wearing any other make-up. She hadn't even tried to conceal the bags under her eyes.

It's like she's proud of them or something.

I scoped out her clothes. While Seth wore Diesel jeans and a pressed Superdry shirt, the girl wore faded, ripped low riders of no particular label in a style that had gone out of fashion two years ago. One tight top was layered over another in a way that almost, but didn't quite, hide an ancient stain and she displayed a tarnished silver necklace in the shape of a dragon. I glanced at her hands and saw that she wore silver rings on every finger, even her thumbs.

The anger faded from her eyes and she appraised me just as openly. There was silence for a beat then she raised her eyebrows. She didn't hold out a hand, but gestured to herself with one thumb. 'I'm Pandra.'

'Cassie.'

'The Doctor said you were coming. You're in the room next to mine. I'll show you.'

Seth stepped forward and the atmosphere thickened. 'Then you can take the bag.' There was open hostility in his voice.

Pandra sneered. 'I don't do baggage.'

'It's okay. I'll carry it.' I tried to take the bag from Seth, but he lifted it out of my reach.

'Let's just go.' He glared at Pandra's retreating back. It was obvious something had gone on between the two of them. My stomach lurched unhappily and I stomped the feeling down.

I shouldn't jump to conclusions, and anyway, why should I care?

Pandra halted outside a closed door. 'This is you.' She rapped the wood with a closed fist. 'Come and say hi once you're settled.'

She disappeared into the room next to mine. As her door closed I tried, and failed, to see inside. When I turned back I realised the whole party had watched her go, including Seth. She drew attention like a wasp at a picnic.

I shook my head and pushed my own door. Nothing happened.

'Here.' Seth handed me a smooth white card. 'This is your key.

It acts like a credit card too, for meals and other stuff. There are some things you can do to get credit added to it, if you want.'

Sure enough there was a slot in the frame. With fingers that trembled only a little I used the card to enter the room that would be my home from now on.

Weak rain-light poured in through the barred windows and striped the white bedding. My gaze followed the lines of shadow to the shafts embedded in the sill and I pulled at my collar, which suddenly felt much too tight. 'It looks like a prison cell.'

Mum stroked my ponytail, a gesture she hadn't made in a long time. 'It'll be alright. Look there's a DVD player; we'll post you some films.'

Seth dumped my bag on the bed. 'You can borrow some of mine while you wait, if you like.'

I was sceptical. 'What have you got?'

'You think I wake up in the night and watch *Alien vs. Predator*? It's all light entertainment.' He gave me an unreadable look. 'You can come and take a look later.'

Mum huffed and Seth backed towards the door, talking rapidly. 'I'd better tell you the rules: we're allowed to mix in each other's rooms during the day but, from nine p.m., boys and girls remain in their own wings. The treatment area is off limits unless you have an appointment. You'll find your schedule in the folder on your desk.'

He stopped with his back to the door. 'There're two buttons in the unit beside your bed. The red one is a panic button – if you wake up in the night and need help you can press it. The night nurse will come in, turn on the light for you, whatever.' He was feigning nonchalance but his eyes had darkened.

'What about the other button?'

His lips thinned. 'The white one connects to a recorder. When you wake in the night you have to press that button and record everything you can remember from your dreams.'

'Are you serious?' My own breath trembled in my ears as Seth exhaled.

'I know . . . it's horrible. You want to think about something else, not relive the storyline. But it's an important part of the treatment.' He tensed. 'If the Doctor finds a tape empty in the morning, she wants to know why.'

I wanted to ask more. I didn't know when I'd next be able to speak to him, and I wanted to make the most of my chance, but Mum slammed my suitcase open meaningfully.

'I'll give you the full tour another time.' Seth backed into the corridor and the closing door shut him off. I glanced at the barred window again. I was inside the Doctor's treatment centre, but I was not alone.

For the first time since I'd spoken to the police about Zillah's grave my spirits started to rise.

CHAPTER EIGHT

TREATMENT

An hour later Mum had hung all my clothes in the small wardrobe, laid my toiletries out in the tiny en-suite bathroom and run out of reasons to stay. Dad had spent the time on the single armchair, the treatment schedule open on his lap.

Finally, as if her batteries had run down, Mum stopped.

My heart clenched. 'I'll be okay, you know.'

Mum nodded and Dad crossed the floor to her. 'Come on, Marie, she's here to get better and that's what'll happen.' He flicked his fingers towards the folder and spoke to me. 'Some of these treatments are going to be hard on you, love, but if you were going to get better quickly and easily, you'd have done it years ago. We'd have made sure of it.' He lowered his voice. 'You're strong enough to have coped with the nightmares all this time so we know you can face this.' He gave Mum a shake and she responded with a tiny nod. 'We topped up your mobile but it doesn't look like you'll get any reception here, so you'll need to call from the payphone downstairs. You can phone us any time, day or night, and we can be here in a few hours, if you really need us.'

His tone didn't match his words.

He expects me to get better, not call him in the middle of the night.

I stared at a spot on the floor. 'I'm sure I'll be fine. If you want to be home by dark, you should go.'

Dad nodded but Mum opened her handbag. 'Here. I noticed you didn't pack him . . . but . . .'

She's brought Bunny! I hesitated before holding out my hand. *I thought it'd be embarrassing to have a cuddly toy with me, but . . . maybe it'll be good to have him tonight.*

'Th-thanks, Mum.' I seized my old toy and my stomach unfurled a little.

After they'd gone I went to the desk and flipped the plastic folder open. I had a booking-in appointment with the Doctor at four p.m. A stainless steel clock ticked quietly on the wall. I had an hour.

Pandra's door swung open when I knocked. The girl lounged on the bed, one leg up, graceful as a model. She was reading Stephen King's *The Stand*.

I paused awkwardly in the doorway. 'How can you read that stuff?'

Pandra shrugged. 'I get the dreams either way.' She bent the spine to mark her place and discarded the book. 'The olds have gone?'

I nodded and stared. The room was a mirror image of mine, but Pandra had obviously been in hers a lot longer. The wall was completely papered with drawings. They were mostly violent and disturbing and many featured the same cast of characters.

One portrait stood out above the others: the pencil strokes, which ranged from near invisibility to angry slashes of black, created a woman so lifelike she seemed three-dimensional. The paper cut her off at the chest, but one hand was in frame because she held a gun to the underside of her chin. The torment in her eyes was so real her hand seemed to shake.

Mesmerised, I drifted towards the picture but didn't touch the paper, afraid of smudging it. I cut my eyes to Pandra. 'Did you draw this?'

She shrugged as if indifferent, but a glimmer in her eyes told me she was pleased by my reaction. 'She doesn't do it.'

I was drawn back to the image. The woman had been battered. Her old-fashioned hairstyle was dishevelled and bruises shadowed her face and chest. Squinting closer I thought I could see what looked like bite marks on her shoulder. The hairs stiffened on the back of my neck. 'Who was she?'

Pandra frowned. 'Her name was Madge . . . Madge . . . something.'

My fingers curled. 'She doesn't shoot herself?'

Pandra shook her head. 'I stopped her.'

My eyes went back to the picture and I rubbed the goose bumps that had appeared on my arms. 'You stopped her.'

'In my last life.' The other girl curled her long legs under her and toyed with the bar pinned through her eyebrow. 'You know, everyone we dream about is dead. Not one of them can be hurt any more. Sometimes knowing that is all that gets me through the night.' She gestured at the macabre wallpaper. 'When I wake up and all I can see is this stuff I remember they're long gone . . . so there's no point torturing myself.'

I sank on to her mattress, eyes still on the portrait. 'Do you really believe the people we dream about don't matter because they're dead?' I looked at her.

She twisted the rings on her left hand as she answered. 'Course. The Doctor's really big on helping us let go of guilt that doesn't belong to us.'

Mention of the Doctor made me check Pandra's clock. It was almost buried by the sheets of paper that were crammed on to every available space. An image of a dragon covered the twelve. Oddly out of place, it was painted with acrylics so bright it appeared to writhe on the paper.

'I've got an appointment at four.' My head throbbed with a full-blown tension headache and I winced. 'Have you got any paracetamol?'

Pandra's leg nudged mine. 'We aren't allowed to "self-medicate" here.' Her eyes flicked to the door and her hand slid under her mattress. 'I haven't got anything to give you.' Her wrist moved back and forth as she felt around and came out with a plain white packet. 'Not even any paracetamol.' She handed me the box with a wink.

'Thanks,' I mouthed, and gratefully dry-swallowed two of the tablets. I gagged slightly but got them down. Then I frowned.

Does Pandra think someone's listening in on us?

I didn't dare ask. Returning the packet to her, I looked at her artwork once more. Sitting in the centre was almost like being inside one of the girl's dreams and I was suddenly desperate to be out of the room. 'I'd better go.'

Pandra picked up her book. 'You'll sit with me at tea?' Surprised, I nodded and her blue eyes flashed. 'Good luck then.'

As I backed out of Pandra's room I nearly bumped into Seth loping down the corridor. At the sight of him bubbles of excitement burst in my gut and I tried to smooth down my hair.

When he saw where I'd been a flush darkened the skin around his scar, but all he said was, 'I'm to make sure you don't miss your first appointment.'

'I was just on my way.'

We fell into step and he cleared his throat. 'Pandra's been here longer than any of us. I don't know what she was like before, but now she's . . . I guess you could say, indoctrinated?'

'She was nice to me.'

'I'm sure she was.'

Seth halted just in front of the swinging door above the staircase. I stopped next to him and, kind of horrified at my own behaviour, leaned in until I could smell his spicy deodorant and the washing powder used on his shirt.

He huffed under his breath. Then he looked at me. 'Don't get me wrong, we're all here to be cured, or at least to find a way to live with what's going on up here.' He tapped his forehead. 'That means we need to listen to the Doctor. But you have to think carefully about some of the things she says to you. Pandra too. Don't just take all their ideas straight to heart, okay?'

I nodded slowly, but knew my face gave away my confusion.

He sighed. 'For Pandra, whatever the Doctor says is gospel, but some truths are more true than others.' He winced. 'Am I making any sense?'

'I guess so.' I examined my fingernails and considered what Pandra had said to me: that the people we dreamed about could no longer come to harm. Maybe that was true for her, but to me the hurt felt real and Karla's suicide proved that our past lives did have consequences. I hesitated. Discussing reincarnation as if it was something other than fantasy was so surreal.

'D-do you have a past life too?' I half covered my mouth as if I could take my words back if Seth laughed at me.

Seth checked his watch then rested against the wall. 'Past lives, Cassie, same as you,' he replied.

I dropped my hand from my mouth. 'So . . . you do remember more than one past life.'

Seth's mouth sank into a sad line. 'We all do. The most recent life is usually the one that affects us most strongly, but not always.'

'It isn't?'

He shook his head. 'You remember Kyle?' I nodded; the rocker with the green eyes was hard to forget. 'He says his clearest memories are from the building of the pyramids at Giza.'

'You're kidding!'

Seth offered a twist of a smile. 'I think our strongest memories are either from the most recent or the most violent and eventful lives . . . but I could be wrong.'

I glanced at his scar. 'Somehow I don't think many of our past lives have been calm or uneventful.'

'You're probably right.' Seth twitched his hair to cover the puckered skin and I looked awkwardly away.

'I wonder why we're the only ones who remember our past lives. If everyone's lived before I mean.' I thought resentfully of my roommate in Germany and how peacefully she'd slept.

'I've thought about that.' Seth's palm rasped over the hint of stubble that just shadowed his cheeks. 'I don't think *everyone* reincarnates. If souls were just recycled all the time, populations wouldn't be able to grow.'

'That actually does make sense. But why are *we* reincarnating if no one else does?'

Seth shook his head. 'I asked the same question. The Doctor thinks some people are destined to live out "little" lives.' He raised two fingers for the word 'little' and emphasised it as he spoke. 'They're born, they die and it doesn't really matter. Except to the people around them, I suppose.' He spread his hands. 'She thinks others are born to do certain things, to fulfil a destiny, like history needs them to or something. She thinks those souls are reborn over and over until they fulfil that destiny.'

'What . . . like I'm meant to do something great and I'll keep coming back till I get it right?'

'Not necessarily something great.' Seth's nose twitched as if he wasn't sure about his own words. 'Just something important. There must be lots of things important to history that don't seem that special at the time.'

'And you believe this?'

Seth crossed his arms. 'It's as good an explanation as any.' His eyes locked on mine then he peeled himself off the wall. 'Come on,' he said. 'We can talk more about this stuff later. You don't want to be late for an appointment with the Doctor. Believe me.'

He walked me down the staircase. 'Go to the end of the corridor and sit on one of the chairs there. You won't need to knock; she'll expect you to be on time.'

I nodded dumbly.

'Go on, you've only got a few minutes.' Seth nudged me towards the doors and turned towards the leisure centre.

As he left apprehension settled in my belly like gristle. The double doors looked innocent enough, but the sign by them – *Treatment Area* – shone a sickly green in the light reflected from the carpet and seemed to warn me against entering.

When I placed my hands on the doors I almost expected them to resist my weight. Instead they swung open and I had no reason not to walk into the corridor.

This is my first step towards losing Zillah. I should be happy.

But my feet dragged on the carpet and the indigestible mass of anxiety grew.

According to my watch, I'd been sitting outside the Doctor's office for five minutes. It felt like much longer; enough time for my knotted stomach to tighten. I rubbed my chest, attempting to relieve the acid round my heart, and tried not to think about the coming appointment. But there were no distractions in the waiting area, nothing to look at: no pictures, not even a scuff pattern in the paintwork.

Finally I decided to ignore Seth's advice and knocked. There was no sound from inside. I pressed my ear against the door and heard no call to enter. Perhaps the Doctor had forgotten my appointment.

What if she isn't even there?

I bounced on my toes, snatched a breath and turned the handle. The door swung open in churchlike silence. Inside the office, a carbon copy of the one in London, the Doctor sat at her desk absorbed in a large book.

With an expression of intense concentration she made a note on the text.

Curiosity propelled me into the room . . . and my nightmare burst into life.

The office faded into the background. All I could see was the book on the desk and there was no doubt: it was the same book I had seen in the most terrifying of my new nightmares.

Unable to resist its pull, I stepped nearer.

My feet scraped the carpet and the Doctor looked up.

Immediately she covered the pages in front of her and jumped to her feet.

I stumbled backwards out of the room. The Doctor pursued me as far as the doorway. There she stopped and throttled the frame with fingers so white I thought they would splinter the wood. 'You *never* enter this office without permission, Miss Smith. Wait here until I fetch you.'

The door thudded closed and I gasped as if I was drowning. The air felt too thin and I couldn't catch my breath.

When the Doctor finally reappeared and gestured me into the room I lowered my eyes, not wanting her to see the fear in them.

Gingerly I sat in the chair meant for me. There was no sign of the book anywhere. Instead a silver laptop whirred on the desk as if such old-fashioned things no longer even existed.

I jumped and half turned as the Doctor placed her hand on the chair back. Sitting, my head barely reached the tops of her legs.

She was first to break the strained silence. 'I'm glad your parents finally decided to send you to us, Cassie.'

The Doctor's lipstick was bright red and I shivered, unable to dismiss the sense that she had a rim of blood round her mouth. I forced a smile and she took her place on the opposite side of the desk.

'I hope you're settling in alright? You've met Pandra? You're the same age, so I thought you'd appreciate being next door.'

I nodded, saw the Doctor's eyes narrow and knew she expected more of a response from me. 'Thanks,' I murmured.

'You saw her artwork?' It sounded like a question, but it wasn't. *The Doctor knows I was in Pandra's room.*

I nodded again and the Doctor glanced at her computer screen. 'Pandra's a very talented artist. Please make use of the art facilities in the leisure area yourself. If you can find some way of getting your dreams out of your head and into reality it would help us both a great deal.' Her tongue flicked over her lips. 'Allowing me to see what you are seeing can only move our sessions along faster. You will also discover that such an outlet is cathartic. You may find that your nightmares abate a little if you can pin them on to paper.'

Instantly I resolved to experiment as soon as I could. I drummed my fingers on the arms of the chair. 'What do the others do?'

The Doctor tilted her head. 'Have you met Lenny?'

I shook my head. 'I've met Kyle and Seth.'

'Ah, well. Seth sculpts magnificently. Kyle's genius is music. He knows everything about musical history and theory, he composes and he plays several instruments. He puts his dreams into music. Not as explicitly useful to me as the other talents, but quite amazing nevertheless.' She paused. 'I've found that all of you tend to do something exceptional, as though you've had several lifetimes to perfect it.' Her eyes snapped to mine and I froze. 'Do you?'

'Do I . . . what?'

'Have such a talent?'

With a sinking heart I thought about my lack of skill in the school art department and shook my head. The Doctor released me from her gaze. 'Maybe you've just not had the chance to discover it. Try some things out and see what comes naturally.'

She typed in silence for a moment then continued. 'The leisure areas are all open to you of course, but if you decide to go outside please keep to the Manor grounds. There are a number of rivers and streams in the surrounding area and we tend to get flash floods at this time of year. The road has been washed out more than once and the moor can be quite dangerous.'

'Floods . . .' I echoed.

'Yes, I believe one of the locals drowned a couple of years ago.'
She paused. 'You'll be fine as long as you stick to the grounds . . .
and I can think of no reason for you to leave them.'

I nodded, but my cheeks were cold.

The Doctor's fingers twitched and she leaned forward. 'I
understand Seth has filled you in on our rules. The only other
thing I must insist on is that you stick to your treatment schedule.'
She licked her lips. 'Which I'm sure you will. Now . . . I think you
should know that I've had time to verify your story with the
German police.'

At her words I jumped and looked behind me, half expecting
to find an officer standing there.

The Doctor smiled briefly. 'I managed to do so without
revealing your identity, although I may not be able to hold them
off forever. If you cooperate with your treatment, I'll speak to
them on your behalf so you aren't investigated.'

'Investigated?' My voice was faint.

*It'll get in the papers. I'll never live it down . . . never get a job . . .
and what about Mum and Dad?*

I forced my shoulders to relax.

The Doctor will keep me anonymous. All I have to do is cooperate . . . and get Zillah out of my head.

The Doctor leaned forward again. 'For our first session, I would like to ask you a few questions under hypnosis.'

My eyebrows shot upwards.

'You don't believe in hypnosis?'

'I've seen Paul McKenna on TV. I-it's just . . .'

'You don't think you'll be a good subject. I've heard it all before and I don't anticipate any problems with you, Cassie.'

I grimaced. There was no way I'd relax enough to go under. Despite my plan to cooperate I didn't want to give the Doctor that much control.

She stood in front of me and her legs trapped me in place like the bars on the windows. Then she reached round the back of my chair and tipped me back. 'Just relax.'

Off balance and disorientated I met her cold blue eyes.

Like a dying candle my thoughts flickered: *That was fast.* The part of me I thought of as Cassie Farrier fought to retain awareness.

She failed.

CHAPTER NINE

INTRODUCTIONS

L ate for dinner; I sat alone in the dining room. I'd missed Pandra, but didn't have the energy to worry about it.

Physically I was alright, better in fact than I had been in some time, as if I'd got a few hours' sleep. Mentally, though, I felt fuzzy, as I did after a nightmare. I wished I knew what had happened while I was hypnotised, but the Doctor had refused to tell me.

Dully I stared at the bottle in my hand. I had been instructed to take the tablets two at a time with my evening meals. I sighed and although I didn't know what they were I reached for my water and downed the light blue capsules.

I wasn't hungry, but the tablets weren't to be taken on an empty stomach. I lifted a cooling chip in my fingers and chewed. It tasted like cardboard.

A hand landed on my shoulder and my tray rattled as I spun round. It was Seth and he wasn't alone; a strange boy and girl stood next to him.

It took a moment for me to process that there was no threat

then I dropped the few inches back to my seat. Only then did I realise that I was gripping my knife. I didn't remember picking it up. I frowned and laid it down with a click.

'We've come to check on you,' the girl said, with the barest flicker of her eyes to the knife that now lay by my plate. 'The first session's heavy going. You'll get used to it.'

She appeared to be a couple of years younger than I was, but that might have been because she was wearing a short dress with patterned tights. Pale mid-length blonde hair was pinned away from her face with hairclips shaped like butterflies. Her cornflower-blue eyes, however, were hooded and ancient, telling me nothing of her true age. I wondered who she had been in her last life.

'I'm Belinda.' She sat opposite me then waited, haughty as a princess, until the other boy rushed to push her chair in, so occupied in his task that he barely glanced at me.

Seth smiled as boy pulled his own chair as close to Belinda's as the table would allow. 'That's Maxwell, Max to you and me.' He slid into the vacant seat on my left and rubbed his eyes. 'So, how are you feeling?'

I reached for another chip and tried to calm my shaking. 'Like I've been in the ring with Triple-H.'

Max gaped, finally seeing me. 'You know wrestling?'

It took me a moment to process both his question and his accent: he was American.

I blinked. 'Sure, it's fun. More like acrobatics than fighting.' I chewed on my lip. 'It's odd. I can't watch anything scary; no war films, nothing violent, but I can watch WWE and TNA.' I paused, mugged by memory. 'I used to watch with my dad when I was smaller. That's how I got into it.'

Max shoved back a blond mop of a fringe and grinned. 'That's rad. I like Cena but you gotta love the Undertaker.'

I snorted. 'No one'll ever come close to the Rock.'

'He was awesome, but you should live in the now.'

The gentle sparring was taking my mind off the previous couple of hours so I dived gratefully into the conversation. I'd never really had friends before.

When I'd finished dinner the others took me to the rec room. In one corner I recognised Kyle. He leaned into another girl, but I could see nothing of her except a frizz of curl that bounced along with her loud brays of laughter. Seth's jaw jutted. 'That's Lizzie. Excuse me a minute.'

Half of my attention remained with him as Belinda and Max herded me to the table football.

'Right, Lizzie, give me your mobile,' snapped Seth.

The girl looked up. She was barely into her teens, yet Seth's firm tone obviously didn't bother her. She raised untamed eyebrows at him. 'No chance.' Her round face assumed stubborn lines.

'I met Kyle leaving Pandra's room, so I know you were taking pictures in mine.'

Lizzie huffed. 'Huh. I lost this round of Double Dares. Kyle got into Pandra's room because she left her door ajar while she was on the loo. I couldn't get into your room. Those locks are way too secure.'

I caught Belinda's eye. She was listening to the exchange just like I was.

Seth glanced at the clock with a frown. 'Where's Lenny? He never misses *The Simpsons.*'

Lizzie's face blanched and Kyle lurched out of his chair. '*The pool!* We didn't know what time it was, honest, man.'

The others ran after him towards the door, but I remained by the football table. Belinda turned with a swish of pale hair.

'Cassie? You won't want to miss this.'

I gritted my teeth. I *hated* swimming pools: the smell of chlorine made me sick. But I'd only just started to fit in here. Dragging my feet I weaved tiredly after them and wondered absently why everyone was so worried that this Lenny had gone swimming.

The entrance to the pool was along a corridor that absorbed noise like a muffler.

The door ahead had closed behind Max. I leaned forward without touching it and peered through the panel set in the woodwork. On the ceiling the pool's reflection blended surreally with a painted starscape and the whole room had a blue tinge. Even standing by the poolside it would be like looking at the sky from underwater . . .

. . . *as if you'd drowned.*

'What's going on?' Feet ruffled the carpet behind me and I turned.

Pandra was marching towards me, her piercings glittering under the fluorescent lights. A towel was slung over her shoulders and she held her key card ready.

'Pandra . . .' I started to apologise for missing dinner, but she overrode me.

'Why are you just standing there? Is the pool closed?' Her face clouded and I automatically took a step backwards before shaking my head.

She reached past me, swiped her card and assaulted the door. 'In or out?'

'In . . . I guess.'

The smell of chlorine brought the memories back.

Mum had booked my first swimming lesson when I was five. I'd emerged from the changing rooms, proudly wearing my new swimsuit and shiny orange armbands. Then I'd seen the pool. Mum ended up with bruises and two lifeguards had to carry me out.

She'd tried to get me over my terror of drowning but, the closest I'd ever come to swimming was putting my feet in the paddling pool on Jesus Green. Even then I would only go in if someone held my hand.

Lots of people had phobias. Compared to the dreams my irrational fear had never really worried me.

But now the hum of the filter filled me with dizzying nausea and I stumbled backwards until I leaned against the wall. There I pressed my hands against the tiles.

I'm safe. There's no way I can fall in from back here.

The constant lapping made the pool seem alive; it was as if the water was calling to me. I shuddered and only realised I was staring when Pandra burst out laughing.

Alarmed, I jerked my head up but she wasn't laughing at me. Her attention was at the other end of the pool.

Lizzie and Kyle stood flanked by Max and a faintly cheerful-looking Belinda. Seth stood apart from them beneath a three-tiered diving platform; his face was turned to the ceiling so I followed his gaze.

On the top tier lay a boy with his arms wrapped so tightly around the board his muscles stood out like pebbles. Ginger hair bristled from his head and clashed with skin that even I could see was blue with cold.

'Is *that* Lenny?' My voice echoed from the rippling ceiling.

Pandra threw her towel on to a bench and started forward. 'Yeah, that's Lenny.'

Gritting my teeth I edged after Pandra. Once we were closer

I could hear Seth speaking gently. 'Come on, Lenny, it isn't as high as it looks. If you don't want to jump, you can wriggle back to the steps.'

A steady, unrelenting whimper came from above. 'I can't.'

I looked at the distance he had to fall before he would hit the water and damp air chlorinated my throat. 'H-how long's he been up there?'

Belinda flicked her hair over her shoulder. 'At least two hours.'

'Two hours? We have to get him down. Shouldn't we call a nurse or . . . something?'

Kyle shook his head. 'No! Not yet. Give Seth a chance.' He flushed. 'He wanted to play Double Dares. Lizzie told him if he wanted to play he had to jump from the highest board. We didn't think he'd actually try and do it. Oh, man.' He grabbed Lizzie's hand. 'The Doctor's gonna kill us.' Dismay bleached his voice.

Pandra muttered under her breath, kicked off her shoes and began to climb the ladder.

'Not a good idea.' Seth reached for her, but she clambered out of reach.

'This is my swim time,' she snapped.

Mesmerised I watched her reach the top and stand; a slim figure outlined against the cobalt ceiling. Her earrings glittered like the Orion's Belt painted above her head.

Then I heard her voice. 'Last chance, Lenny. Get back here or you're going off the end.'

'No.' The reedy reply rang loudly and petulantly.

'Fine,' she snapped, and took a single step on to the springboard.

'Pandra, what are you doing?' Seth shouted, and leaped towards the ladder, but before he could place his foot on the first rung, she had jumped in place.

My heart slammed inside my chest. Lenny screeched and she jumped again. The board shuddered: she was going to shake him off. I collapsed on to a bench.

She could've just pulled him back.

With a howl, Lenny tried to lock his ankles together. He failed. Shrieking, he flew upwards. Then he bounced wildly from the end of the board and flipped towards the pool.

He'll drown!

Lenny was still in mid-air when water splashed my face. I jerked and saw Seth, fully dressed, stroking towards the deep end.

I gripped the bench as Lenny slammed into the surface. His

impact washed a wave all the way to my feet. Immediately Seth dived to intercept him.

After what seemed an eternity the two of them came back up. Seth shouted at Lenny to stop struggling and pulled him to the edge by his shoulders.

Only then did I turn my eyes back to the diving board. Once Lenny had been removed Pandra had apparently lost interest in the drama and shucked her clothing. She posed in a red Speedo swimsuit, waved at me then dived fearlessly into the pool.

'Someone help me out here.' Seth was half balanced on the poolside, trying to keep Lenny's head above water.

Max pulled the squirming youngster up by his wrists and as soon as Lenny was safe on the tiles Seth pulled himself out of the pool. Coils of black hair had escaped from the elastic that held it back and as he rose to his knees strands trailed across his shoulders and stuck to his shirt like seaweed.

He sagged, water dripping from his nose. 'Is he alright?'

Max gave him a nod. 'He's cold and a bit bruised, but basically okay.'

'I'm not okay.' The boy was sitting up now, his arms wrapped round his toast-rack chest. 'I'm *telling on you*, Lizzie.' His nasal voice spiralled upwards and he coughed snot on to Max's trousers. 'This is *your fault.*'

The sound of his voice wound like wire into my ears and I twitched, lifting one shoulder as if I could scrub it from my hearing.

'You didn't have to do it, Lenny.' Lizzie was nearly hysterical. 'You can't tell. They might kick me off the programme.'

'Good.'

In the pool Pandra continued to do graceful laps while Belinda, Max and Kyle clustered around Lenny, begging him to stay quiet.

It's nothing to do with me.

My eyes met Seth's; he too was staying back. He leaned on his elbows, his attitude one of exhausted annoyance.

Turning to hide my blush I noticed Lenny's pile of clothing, along with the key card he must have used to get into the pool.

Didn't that mean the nurses knew where he was? Surely after an hour someone should have checked on him . . .

With a prickle of foreboding I peered around until I located the security camera in the right-hand corner of the ceiling.

Why hadn't anyone come to help?

CHAPTER TEN

SETH

'I need to change.' Seth climbed to his feet and water pooled around his trainers. 'Lizzie, Kyle, no more Double Dares for a while. Lenny, just drop it.'

Lizzie and Kyle nodded, shamefaced, but Lenny opened his mouth in a long-noted wail. 'That's *not fair.*'

My eyebrows climbed.

He isn't even going to say thanks.

Seth ignored the whining and turned to me. 'You want to come get some DVDs?' He tapped his sodden wristwatch; an expensive-looking Tag Heuer. 'You'll need to do it now if you want them for tonight.'

Grateful for a reason to leave I nodded enthusiastically. 'That'd be great.'

He headed for the exit and I followed, careful to keep my gaze from the churning water.

As I took the weight of the door and stepped into the corridor the nagging pressure of eyes on my back made me turn. Pandra was leaning on the rail glaring at our retreat. Shocked at the hostility on her face I dropped the door.

It crashed into the frame and Seth spun round. Instantly his hands flew up to cover his head. '*Gotenu!*'

'Seth?' I reached for his shoulder, but he dropped into a defensive crouch and batted my hand away. Confusion forced me back towards the pool.

What did I do wrong?

The door flew open behind me. 'Get away from him, Cassie.' Max hurried into the corridor.

'W-why? What's going on?'

Belinda caught up. 'Did it set him off?'

'Yeah.' Max tore his gaze from Belinda so he could speak to me. 'Just leave him for a few minutes.'

Seth huddled against the wall. My arms ached to go round his shoulders, but I held them at my sides. 'I don't understand.' Frantically I looked for the threat. 'What's happening?'

Belinda regarded me coldly. 'Think about it. Why are we all here?' I stared blankly and she looked at me as if I was stupid. 'It's one of his past personalities.' She gestured towards Lizzie, Kyle and Lenny who were still arguing by the swimming pool. 'It happens to us all.'

'B-but everyone else seems okay.'

Max licked his lips. 'We all have different triggers. Lenny's is heights. That's why he shouldn't have been on that board. Seth's is loud noises. The banging door set him off.'

'Seth?' He gave no sign that he'd heard my whisper and I bit my cheek.

Max looked sympathetic. 'He'll be alright. When it happens to you, you'll understand.'

I took an involuntary step backwards. 'It won't happen to me. It never has.'

Belinda's lips curled into an ugly smile. 'Now you're here, it will.'

I wanted to argue, but movement from Seth stole my voice. He rubbed his face and when his palms came away his eyes were clear. 'Dammit.' He set his jaw and I tried to stammer an apology but he waved it away. 'You weren't to know.'

'Yes, but . . .'

'I don't want to talk about it.' His eyes pleaded with me to let it go. 'Do you still want those DVDs?' He shuffled his feet. 'Or maybe you won't want to come with me now.'

Chilled, I rubbed my elbows. Seth's uncertainty made him seem less like the person I'd been coming to know. Suddenly I wondered how much of that person was really him and how much some ghost.

I couldn't think straight, so I just followed my instincts. 'Of course I want to come.'

Seth said nothing as we climbed the stairs but when we neared his room my memory of Pandra's angry face intruded.

If she thinks I'm moving in on her territory, she might turn on me.

Much as I wanted to get closer to Seth, I didn't want to upset Pandra doing it. I had to ask an awkward question. I squirmed. 'Um, Seth w-what went on with you and Pandra?'

Seth must have been expecting me to ask about his transformation. His shoulders relaxed. 'Me . . . and Pandra?'

Embarrassment coloured my cheeks, but I pushed on. 'She doesn't seem to like me spending time with you . . . so, you know, I just wondered . . . were you boyfriend and girlfriend or something?'

'God no, nothing like that. It's just that she pretty much hates me and, right now, she likes you.'

'That's it?' My voice rose.

Seth dragged his key card through the slot by his door. 'When Pandra takes against someone she *really* does. There's nothing half-hearted with her.' His voice held grudging respect. 'I don't actually know why she hates me, but I'm on that list, alongside her real parents and a few others.'

I cast a quick glance behind us as if she would hear us gossiping. 'Her real parents?'

'It's no secret, she'll tell you herself if you ask her, but you might not want to wind her up.' He paused with one hand on his doorplate. 'Pandra's a scholarship case. She's been in and out of foster homes all her life. Her last family used to watch one of those paranormal TV shows. Pandra saw the Doctor and tracked her down. I think she's been here ever since.'

'Ever since . . .' Seth made it sound like Pandra had been in Mount Hermon forever. 'How long ago was that?'

'Not sure exactly, she was here when I arrived.' He shrugged. 'From what she told me when we were still speaking, I know it's been over a year.'

'A year! I thought I'd be home in a few weeks.'

Seth's eyes crinkled. I couldn't tell if he was sympathetic, or marvelling at my stupidity. 'It'll take more than a few weeks, but remember . . . Pandra has nowhere else to go.'

My fingers felt numb and I flexed my hands. 'The Doctor lets her stay for free then.' I thought about my own parents and the crippling financial agreement they'd had to sign.

Seth waved in the vague direction of the treatment rooms. 'I think she's agreed to all sorts of experimental therapies. To the Doctor she's a sort of lab rat-cum-book subject, crossed with a surrogate daughter. Did the Doctor tell you how pleased she is with Pandra's progress?'

I nodded but my mind raced. 'So . . . she sees her like a daughter but does experimental treatments on her . . .'

Seth's lips narrowed. 'I'm not sure the Doctor sees things like you and me.' He looked around almost surreptitiously. 'I'm not sure she feels things the same way either.'

We regarded each other silently and the shadows in his eyes seemed to deepen. Then he shook himself free and opened his door. 'Ignore the mess,' he said.

Inside, Seth headed for the bathroom, already toeing off his trainers and peeling his shirt over his head. The remains of his ponytail pulled free and slapped on to his spine. The cold water had bleached his skin but a sprinkle of coffee-coloured freckles tapered towards his waist. Quickly I averted my eyes.

'Make yourself at home,' he called, to the sound of water-logged denim hitting the bathroom floor.

I glanced at the chair, which was piled high with laundry, and opted to sit on the bed. Seth emerged a few minutes later with a blue towel round his waist.

A striped dressing gown lay in a corner. He swept it up, swung it round his shoulders and yanked the belt tight. Then he dropped on to the mattress next to me. His leg did not quite touch mine, but I could feel the heat of it even through the double layer of towelling.

My little finger twitched as if to touch him but I held it still. I didn't dare raise my eyes to his and my gaze flicked around the room looking for something to rest on.

Suddenly thoughts of Seth's nearness vanished. His dressing gown had been covering two incredible sculptures. Wanting a closer look I rose to my feet.

The first seemed simple. It was a badge cast in stone lying on a clump of turf. The sigil itself was stark, a circle containing seven stars and a sort of broken figure eight. I tilted my head and frowned. 'Is that *Orion*?' The sign seemed to be following me.

Seth followed my eyes. 'It's the shoulder insignia of the Twenty-seventh Division of the US army. The original commander was Major General John O'Ryan. Orion, see?'

I frowned. 'Did *you* make that?' Seth shrugged and I took it to mean that he had.

'Why?' I drifted over to the stone, fingers outstretched.

He watched me touch the sculpture. 'I was in the New York National Guard in my life before last. We all joined the Twenty-seventh in 1917.'

My fingers paused in the act of stroking a blade of grass. 'Is that who you –' I groped for the right words – 'turned into back there?' I gestured in the vague direction of the pool.

Seth shook his head and his knuckles whitened on his lap. 'I don't want to talk about her.' His hand brushed the hair that covered his scar. 'It makes me feel like I used to .. . before.'

'Before what?'

He drew his legs up. 'When I was younger. Look, I really don't want to discuss it.'

He looked so vulnerable that I figured the ghost, whoever she was, still lingered somehow. I looked away, wrestling with the desire to prise more information out of him and my attention went to the other sculpture.

It was brilliant. A beautiful girl was half mired in the stone as if climbing out, or perhaps being absorbed back inside. Instead of filling in every detail, Seth had managed to only hint at certain things: the curve of her eyebrow, the line of her spine, the subtle grace of her fingers. Somehow that made her all the more lifelike. And she was somehow familiar.

'Who's that?'

Seth blushed. 'It's no one. Just a dream.'

I turned from her to him. 'You know, I don't think I've *ever* just dreamed.'

'I know what you mean.' He sagged. 'With all these past lives,

I don't know how much space there is for normal dreams.'

'So maybe she's someone from a past life?'

'Maybe.' He cleared his throat, swung his feet off the bed and headed to his wardrobe. 'Here, take any you like.' He opened the door with a bit of a flourish and I gawked. Despite the carpet of clothes on the floor the wardrobe was stuffed and, beneath the hangers of designer shirts, Seth had a whole library of DVDs.

Then I saw the titles and burst out laughing. 'You weren't kidding when you said you could lend me light entertainment.' I knelt in front of the range and read a few of them out. '*Porkys*? *Ferris Bueller's Day Off*? *American Pie*?'

Seth pursed his lips. 'What were you expecting?' He leaned over my shoulder and grunted as if he was seeing the selection for the first time.

My finger traced the colourful boxes. 'Can I borrow this one?'

He checked my choice and smiled. '*Blackadder*? Sure. One's missing, hang on.'

He rolled over the bed to open his own DVD player and a series-three disc popped out. I slotted it into the box set. 'You're sure you don't mind?'

He shook his head. 'It's not like I've nothing else to watch. I fancy *That 70s Show* tonight anyway.'

I brandished my prize. 'Thanks.'

Seth grimaced. 'I don't know about you, but I never watch the final episode.'

'Series four?' I rubbed my forehead. 'Thanks for reminding me . . . you're right, I shouldn't watch that one.'

Gently Seth's fingers brushed my shoulder. 'Do you ever not dream about death or violence?'

My head felt like lead as I shook it, but at the same time all my nerves seemed to be focused on my shoulder where his fingers still lay, light as feathers.

Suddenly a bell sounded and we both jumped guiltily. Seth checked the clock. 'You'd better go; they'll come and make sure we're all in our own rooms in a bit.' He paused. 'I was just wondering, is Cassie short for something? Cassandra maybe?'

I never told anyone my full name. It was kind of embarrassing. I fiddled with the DVD boxes. 'Mum was into astronomy when she had me . . . It's short for Cassiopeia.'

'That's unusual.' His eyebrows twitched together.

I nodded. 'Did you ever watch *Clash of the Titans* when you were a kid?'

'I loved that film. Cassiopeia was the . . . queen, right?'

'That's right.' I tightened my fingers on the DVD. 'She was punished by the gods. Some say Ethiopia was drowned because of her.' I wrinkled my nose. 'Maybe she wasn't the greatest person to be named after.'

Seth grinned. 'At least she got a constellation. Set in the stars forever, that's not so bad.'

'Yeah.' I raised the DVD. 'Thanks for this.'

'No problem.' He opened his door for me and dropped his voice. 'Sleep well, Cassiopeia.'

'You too,' I murmured.

The futility of the sentiment was lost on neither of us.

CHAPTER ELEVEN
LOHENGRIN

On the way back to my room I almost collided with Lenny.

'Sorry,' I said, forcing a cheerful tone. 'I nearly ran you down. I'm Cassie.'

At the sound of my voice he cringed, then straightened but kept his head at an odd angle as if ready to duck. My hands spontaneously formed fists.

'This is the boy's area. You're not supposed to be here.' His voice grated like fingernails on sheet metal and I had to force my fingers open.

I didn't want to argue with a little kid. 'I'm on my way to my room right now.'

'Huh.' His dirt-grey eyes alighted on the box set and filled with calculation. 'You've been to see Seth, haven't you?' He sidled nearer, rubbing his ginger hair into spikes. 'He won't let me in his room. He won't let me borrow any of his DVDs either. He says they're too old for me. They aren't, though, are they?' He reached for the set in my arms. 'You won't use them all tonight. Can I have some?'

I glanced at the box. 'These are a fifteen; they are too old for you.' I took a step backwards.

Shiftiness dropped over the boy's face like a visor. 'I'll tell. I'll say you were in Seth's room doing *stuff*. That's not allowed here.'

I blushed, betraying myself, and gritted my teeth before I said something I'd regret. Unable to speak, I shouldered past him. Reflexively Lenny bobbed his head and yelped. He sounded like a kicked dog. A blaze of anger drove me halfway back round and I burned with the impulse to really give him something to whine about. He recoiled and I froze.

What am I doing? He's ten years old.

I turned my back on him and ran to my room with the irritating sound of his whining droning in my ears and dizziness bouncing me into the wall.

I fumbled with my key card and slammed through the door, shaking with unreasonable anger.

However, as I cleaned my teeth, tiredness dampened my rage and visions of Seth crowded my mirror. I splashed cold water on my face. It didn't drive away my exhaustion, but it did remind me of the scene outside the pool.

Max's words tolled in my skull: '*When it happens to you, you'll understand*'.

Tomorrow I'll have more treatments and maybe they'll dredge up memories even worse than Zillah's.

I leaned my forehead on the mirror and watched my breath fog the glass until I no longer recognised my reflection. Then I lay face up on the bed and tried to make my mind as blank as the mirror.

When my fingers close round the barrel they're trembling and the sweaty metal almost slips from my hands as I yank the 98k from its place under the seat. Hoping none of the others has noticed my fumbling I swiftly swing the gun round, grip the stock, check the safety catch then pull the stripper clip from my belt. I stroke a round with my thumb before I slide it home. It's so smooth, perfect.

Orders are called from the front of the convoy. I push the stock into my shoulder then line up the sight. I only have five shots before I have to reload, but I'll make every one count.

I dragged myself to breakfast like a week-old corpse and opened the dining room door, feeling sick.

Throughout the night Zillah had visited my dreams over and over again. Each time I recorded the details of her death on the tape recorder; it seemed to breathe new life into her.

However, it was not Zillah who haunted me this morning. I didn't know how the gunman had taken over the nightmare at the last, but I could not rid myself of his face.

Even now his thoughts oozed through my memories like the sludge at the bottom of an old fridge, spoiling everything they touched.

I lowered myself gingerly into my chair, shuddering with the new form the horror had taken.

Pandra dropped into the chair next to me and I had to turn my head with my hands to acknowledge her. She didn't look nearly as bad as I did, though the effort of keeping her eyes open made them water so badly it looked like she was going to cry. She nodded at me and scrubbed her hands through her hair. 'Should be used to this by now,' she muttered.

A scraping sound made me turn and, when I could look, the seat across the table was occupied by Seth.

'Morning,' he rasped. Next to me Pandra actually growled.

I wonder what Seth did to make her hate him so much.

'M-morning.' I ignored Pandra and tried to remember how to speak. 'Thanks for the DVDs.'

Seth shrugged, too exhausted to bother with a reply.

'We need coffee.' Raising her arm Pandra waved at a thickset lady in an apron who hurried over with a steaming pot.

Gratefully I inhaled and after the first couple of sips was able to look around more easily. While I was drinking, the younger residents had stumbled into the dining room and they too were being served coffee for breakfast, even Lenny.

My face cracked into a deep yawn and I jumped as a plate clicked on to the table in front of me.

'Alright, love, d'you want cooked?'

'Cooked?'

'Cooked breakfast. Or there's toast, cereal. What can I get you?'

My stomach turned over. 'Toast, please.' I looked into the face of the waitress. It was shiny with the kitchen's heat. '*Dry* toast.'

She patted my shoulder sympathetically and took orders from Seth and Pandra. Seth was having cornflakes, but Pandra was having a full cooked breakfast, complete with black pudding, sausages, bacon, eggs and beans.

'How *can* you?'

She gave a smile that looked more like a grimace. 'Keeping my strength up.'

'For the extra treatments?'

Pandra's eyes flicked to Seth and her earrings glittered as she turned her head. 'Been talking about me, have you?'

I swallowed. 'Seth mentioned that the Doctor did extra experiments with you.'

Pandra snorted. 'You make me sound like a guinea pig.' She leaned back in her chair. 'I'm making *real* progress because I don't resist *any* of my treatments.' Suddenly she rubbed her eyes. 'I'll admit the experimental stuff can be a bitch some days, but if the Doctor says it'll help I'll do it. She knows what's best.' Her rubbing smeared her kohl, further blackening the smudges under her lashes. She glared at me. 'If you wouldn't do the same, you shouldn't be here.'

I looked at the treacle-dark liquid in my cup. 'Can I ask you something? D-do you use the tape recorder for every dream? After my session the Doctor reminded me to . . . but maybe I misunderstood.'

Gently Seth touched the back of my hand. 'Were your

dreams worse than usual last night?'

'I thought I'd get better once I got here.' I sipped my coffee, trying to calm my frantic heartbeat. 'Last night was so bad I thought maybe I'd done something wrong. Like . . . perhaps you're only supposed to record the first nightmare?' My voice trembled pathetically.

Pandra shook her head. 'We have to record every dream. The Doctor can't help if she doesn't know what you're dreaming about, can she?'

'But what's the point in recording the nightmare over and over?'

Pandra tugged at the dragon on her necklace. 'Maybe the Doctor needs to know how often you have each dream. Maybe she gets a bit more info each time.'

'D-do you dream the same thing every night?'

Pandra looked away from me. 'You've been in my room. You've seen what I dream about.'

I clutched my mug more tightly. 'But . . . you've been here a year. What sort of progress are you making, if you still dream like that?'

Pandra's rings knocked the table as she clenched her fists. 'I'll get there. Right now it's not so much about getting rid of the dreams as addressing my reactions to the dreams.' She gritted her teeth. 'I don't know why I'm telling you this. It's my treatment and I don't want to talk about it any more.'

Seth grimaced. 'We don't talk about our dreams much outside the treatment area, Cass. It's kind of our own unwritten rule. We get enough with the Doctor.'

'Right. Sorry.'

He leaned forward then. 'I can tell you this, though; we all arrived here with a single recurring dream, just like you.' Pandra nodded reluctantly and he continued. 'You already know about Kyle. The nightmare he started with was from ancient Egypt. He's claustrophobic too. *We think* he was bricked inside a tomb.'

My skin pimpled and I rubbed my forearms.

Seth continued. 'Everyone else's first nightmares were from more recent lifetimes. Max . . . well he has visions of Vietnam.'

Pandra's eyes gleamed. 'He spilled some coffee on his hand once and went berserk.'

Seth glowered at her and she fell silent. 'Lizzie dreams about IRA attacks in seventies Belfast. If you ever hear her speaking with an Irish accent, then you should go get help.'

My eyes widened and I looked at the younger girl. She was

giggling with Kyle like any other teenager. My gaze fell on Lenny. He was sitting slightly apart from the others, shoulders hunched. 'What about him?'

'Prisoner of war in Japan. A pilot. Shot down. That's why he hates heights.'

If he dreams about the war, Lenny's dreams must be a bit like mine.

As I dug inside for some fellow feeling I watched him stick his thumb up his nose and flick a knob of snot on to the table. It landed by Belinda's wrist and my eye twitched. She was talking to Max and hadn't noticed Lenny's addition to the tableware. 'What about Belinda?'

It was Pandra who answered. 'The princess was in some kind of race riot.'

Seth nodded. 'Apartheid I think. She hates crowds but, like I said, we don't go for talking about it much. So, yeah, to answer your original question, we all started out dreaming the same thing over and over.'

I was glad I was sitting down. 'Started out?'

He hesitated. 'I'm pretty sure we're all having nightmares about other people now.'

'Since you began the treatment?' I whispered.

Pandra's head dipped into a curt nod and her eyebrow stud flashed.

We said nothing more until our food arrived. The toast piled on my plate looked insurmountable and the smell of Pandra's fried food made me want to throw up. I nibbled at the corner of one crust then dropped it on my plate, defeated.

Pandra looked up with a forkful of bacon halfway to her mouth. 'You can't take the drugs on an empty stomach. Eat something, or the waitress'll report you.'

'Report me?' I stared over at the bustling blonde.

Seth shrugged. 'No one here is quite what they seem. Pam's a nurse too. I expect you'll meet her in one of today's sessions. She's nice enough, but the staff are here to watch us and make sure we stick to the programme.'

With a groan I lifted the toast and put it to my lips. It was like trying to chew plasterboard.

Leaving the dining hall a little while later, however, I found myself humming. It was kind of a rousing tune, which bubbled up inside my throat and wouldn't stop.

Seth snorted. 'You're in a better mood.'

I nodded and continued to hum as I pushed the door open. Suddenly someone else joined in. They had a much nicer voice than I did, but the tune was the same as the one carouselling inside my head. I turned to find Kyle at my elbow. He grinned at me, his green eyes brilliant against the smudges of sleeplessness beneath. 'Hey, man, I've never met anyone else who knew that one.'

'You haven't?'

'Nope. Isn't it great?' Enthusiasm made him babble. 'I don't know why it isn't played more often. How'd you hear it? There are loads of recordings of *Lohengrin*, but that extended version is rare. A friend of my music teacher's let me hear his. It was recorded from an original performance in Bayreuth, 1936.'

My eyes widened. 'Bayreuth . . . 1936?'

Seth caught my elbow but his touch barely registered. 'Kyle,' he warned.

'Yeah, man,' the boy continued blithely. 'Völker just kept going – the crowd went wild. I wish I'd been there.' Finally Kyle looked at Seth. 'Oh, man.' Understanding made him back away. 'Sorry. It's a past life, isn't it? I shouldn't have said anything.' He sprinted for the stairs, a blurred figure all in black, but I barely saw him leave.

How do I have a rare version of some music I've never heard of in my head? It's never been in any of my dreams.

Seth caught my shoulders, steadying me. 'Stuff like this happens here, Cass. It's part of the healing process, getting worse before you get better and all that.'

I shook my head frantically. My chest hurt and I started to gasp. Hands that smelled of washing-up liquid caught my cheeks. 'She's having a panic attack. Help me get her to a treatment room.'

Next thing I knew I was on a couch. There was an oxygen mask over my face and Seth had vanished. The nurse who'd served breakfast remained. She squeezed my hand. 'Alright now?'

'Seth?' I strained my neck, looking for him.

'He had his own treatment to go to.' She lifted my sweat-dampened fringe from my forehead. 'Have a rest. I've checked your schedule – you've an appointment in forty-five minutes so I'll be back in quarter of an hour and we can go over what happened.'

'Okay.' I tried to let my mind go blank but poignant strains of the music continued to float through the blackness.

* * *

'Alright, Cassie, what do you see?'

I was standing in front of a desk covered in greasy metal and polished wood. None of the shapes looked familiar. But, as I stared, an image popped into my head.

Incredulously I pointed at one of the parts. 'Is that a gun barrel?'

The Doctor smiled. Then she folded her arms in a way that drew attention to her biceps. 'Very good, now how do you know that?'

'Cop shows.' This time I had the comfort of knowing that the memory was one of my very own, of sitting with my dad in front of an old TV series.

Hah. No past lives for you there.

She frowned and I pressed my hands together, obscurely pleased to have been able to say that.

'So, what do you think this is?' she asked, gesturing to the table.

My pleasure fled in an uneasy rush. 'Is it . . . bits of a gun?' Abruptly lightheaded I leaned on the table, careful to keep my fingers away from the pieces.

'That's right.' The Doctor was watching my reaction intently. 'I'm going to ask you to do something you might find strange.' She smirked to herself. 'There'll be a lot of that while you're staying here.' She twitched an invisible thread from her starched collar. 'I want you to put the weapon back together.'

'Why?' She might as well have asked me to plunge my arm into a nest of cockroaches. 'I don't want to touch that thing!'

'Need I remind you how important cooperation with your treatment is?' The Doctor loomed over me. 'I was pleased that you managed to record your dreams last night, but I notice that you have yet to visit the art room, as I suggested.'

I swallowed. 'I-I don't see how showing you I don't know how to put a gun together will help me get rid of my nightmares.'

A spot of crimson appeared on each of the Doctor's cheeks and I only then realised how bleached of colour her face usually was. 'You need to become familiar with the objects in your dreams, so that they aren't so frightening. You have to trust me, Cassie. If I have to explain myself to you before every treatment, we aren't going to get very far.'

'I just don't want to touch the gun.' There were tears in my eyes.

'What if I do this?' The Doctor strode across the room towards an iPod in a docking station on the wall. At a gesture from the Doctor music flooded the room.

Kyle had said the recording was rare, but she'd got hold of it in less than an hour. My muscles tightened and I trembled as the notes floated around me.

Then I reached for a piece of the disassembled weapon.

The music vanished and I stood in front of the table with a gun in front of me.

It's a Karabiner 98.

The knowledge floated in the forefront of my memory, then was gone.

The Doctor was looking at me, her eyes glowing. She had a stopwatch in her hand. 'You did that in less than a minute.'

I tottered backwards until I folded on to the chair that had been pushed against the wall. There I stared at the weapon as if it was going to turn on me.

How the hell did I put a gun together?

Chapter Twelve

EMERGENCE

'**W**ell.' The Doctor stroked the edge of the table. 'It seems we've found your talent.'

I shook my head. 'No.'

She nodded towards the gun, needing to add nothing more.

'But I've never even seen a real gun before.'

'Part of you has, and you're beginning to access that knowledge.'

I thought of Zillah and a sob hiccupped from my closed lips.

'What's the matter?'

'Seth gets to sculpt, Kyle's a musician, Pandra draws and what's my special talent?' The words exploded like water from a dam. 'Putting together murder weapons.'

The Doctor fondled the rifle. 'I imagine there's more to it than that. Your talent will extend a long way beyond just assembling a gun, so I'd better have a range built on the grounds.'

My hands tingled and I rubbed them on my thighs. 'You want me to shoot?'

'Although you've not done it before, I believe you'll be an excellent marksman. Do you think Lizzie came here knowing how to carve? She didn't have a clue what a wood veining chisel was, but she picked it up immediately.'

As a wave of dizziness overwhelmed me I clutched my head with one hand and the chair with the other.

How can I even consider *shooting with the same weapon that killed Zillah?*

'I can't do it,' I blustered.

The Doctor raised her eyebrows. 'We can start with other weapons if you prefer.'

'Other weapons?' I blinked.

'Of course. A skill tends to be honed throughout lifetimes. If you're that talented with a gun, you'll have used many more primitive weapons with equal proficiency.'

'Like . . . knives?'

'I expect so, but also a bow, sword, quarterstaff, that sort of thing. I'm going to need to track down an instructor for you to spar with.' She rubbed her hands. 'It isn't the kind of talent that will let me into your head like the others, but it is very interesting.'

* * *

I stumbled out of the office, made my way to one of the casement windows in the rec room and lowered myself on to the bench. I felt as fragile as porcelain.

In a corner of the grounds the tennis courts stood empty. I wondered where the range would be built and thrust my hands under my arms to control the tremors.

Sickened with myself I tried to picture a future that wasn't shaped simply by nightmares and failure.

'What are you *doing*?' The voice was outraged and I jumped.

Did I fall asleep?

I lifted my hand to feel for drool and only then saw the chisel I was holding.

W-where did I get a chisel?

'What are you doing, Cass?' The voice was gentler now and I fought my alarm to look up at Seth.

'I d-don't know.' Flustered, I followed the direction of his appalled glare. Engraved deeply into the stonework of the sill were my initials.

My graffiti had knocked off a piece of carved flower and I covered my mouth with a horrified 'oh'.

His hand was round mine, prising the chisel from my fingers. 'I didn't . . .' I started to protest but Seth's grip was firm.

'Let's get this back to Lizzie's workbench.'

He helped me to my feet and I looked at what I had done. A thrill went through me: *now they'll always know you were here.*

And I was sure the thought wasn't mine.

For a whole week I couldn't even look at the windowsill that bore my initials. I watched the shooting range go up at the end of the grounds, attended increasingly bizarre therapy sessions and started going to the gym. There I ran constantly, attempting to exhaust jags of rage that boiled from nowhere and disappeared as suddenly.

At night I suffered through Zillah's death in ever more vivid detail. Each time I woke I thought the nightmare couldn't get any worse, but each time it became more real until finally, almost inevitably, I started to wake outside of my bed, dazed and wondering who and where I was.

After one nightmare I woke in my bathroom staring into a mirror crazed with a web of cracks. My hairbrush was lying on the floor by my feet and in the fractured reflection my eyes were hysterical.

By the end of the week I felt as if I'd been shipwrecked. Phantom bruises covered my bones. I was exhausted. Moreover, whenever I was alone hopelessness overwhelmed me and drove me to tears.

Surely I'm not meant to feel like this.

I tried to ask the Doctor, but she waved away my concerns.

'You're doing very well. Remember what I said about getting your "ghosts" to realise they're dead and that this lifetime is yours? Well, a part of you is grieving. In the meantime, we need to make sure you release all the guilt you've been carrying for their mistakes.' She licked her lips, slightly smearing her crimson lipstick. 'If you can do this, you can start to experience your nightmares like other people watch horror films. They'll be thrilling, not terrifying.'

'Th-thrilling . . .' My eyes flicked over my hands, seeing a red haze.

Her voice made me raise my head. 'Not all the deaths you are dreaming were your own. It's your guilt that makes you experience them the way you do. You must let go of the remorse.

Embrace the actions you took.' She walked around the desk, automatically avoiding the light fitting that would have brushed the top of her head. Her shadow pinned me against the door. 'I'm very pleased with you, Cassie. Your progress has been excellent.'

'Excellent how?'

'You are opening up to your talent, your most recent past life is close to the surface and so will soon be in a position to accept that your life belongs to you. Furthermore you are unlocking your other past lives with increasing rapidity.'

I nodded dumbly.

It sounds like progress. But it doesn't feel like it.

The Doctor rested her hands on her hips. 'You are aware that Pandra is helping me with additional research.' I nodded even though there was no question in the Doctor's tone. 'I think you would now be a first-rate subject and I'd like you to consider joining one of my experimental programmes.' As alarm altered my face she gestured to the card sticking from my jeans pocket. 'Extra credit would, of course, be added to your account.'

That would help Mum and Dad.

I licked my lips. 'What sort of experimental programme?'

I heard Mum's warning, quiet as a sigh: '*We didn't want you to become a science experiment,*' but the Doctor's reply drowned her out. 'You should know that I am close to a method of eradicating your nightmares.'

Chapter Thirteen

EXPERIMENT

The gun burns and the weight of the barrel bears it downwards. Spent shells litter the ground like autumn leaves; as I take a step forward they clink and roll.

I freeze and for a moment after they stop moving there is silence. Even the birds have fled.

Then the cries of the survivors reach me.

The others gather shovels from the back of one of the trucks, but Hans and I move into the field with our guns.

It is time to clean up.

I jerked awake, freezing cold. The bed was saturated and the room stank.

I've wet myself!

Tears of shame burned in my eyes. With a sob I pressed the red button and immediately a red light blinked on. Someone was coming.

* * *

The next morning I lingered in the bathroom, unwilling to go to breakfast.

Everyone'll know I wet the bed and I can't face being a joke. Not here.

I stared at myself in the mirror.

Maybe if I didn't look so awful . . .

Perhaps it was time to try some of the make-up I bought on the way home from Germany. The little pots and tubes lay in the bottom of my washbag, untouched.

I fiddled with the tube of tinted moisturiser. The lady at the counter had said it would even out my complexion. I dabbed some on. Then I leaned closer to the mirror.

More confident, I applied some pale brown eyeshadow and a slash of lipstick. I considered the near-stranger in the glass, decided the lipstick was one step too far and wiped it off with the back of my hand.

Then I straightened my shoulders and shook out my hair. I'd never look as good as Pandra, but I was ready to face breakfast.

On my way down the hall a nurse stopped me. Embarrassed, I tried to sidestep without meeting his eyes but he caught my shoulder.

'Cassie. The Doctor wants you to go to room 3a rather than her office for this morning's appointment.'

I looked up sharply and the nurse nodded, satisfied I'd got his message. Then he walked away. There was no condemnation on his face. Either he didn't know what had happened to me last night . . .

. . . or he doesn't care. Maybe bed-wetting isn't a big deal here.

At the door marked 3a I stopped and wiped suddenly sweaty palms on my jeans.

Whatever this experiment is . . . if there's any chance the Doctor can get rid of my nightmares, I'm doing it.

I opened the door and had to squint. All around the room fluorescent light reflected from white ceramic tiles. The glare made the room look like a temple of celestial judgement.

One wall was taken up by a large internal window, but as I stepped inside my gaze went directly to the console beneath it.

Although I could only see a single switch and dial, they seemed ominous. The dial was set into a spectrum that ranged from the blue of a swimming pool to the red of clotting blood. As I wondered what it could be for, there was a click.

Swiftly I tried the door. It had locked behind me.

I took a steadying breath, turned back and looked through the window on to another, much larger room.

Although the walls were as white as mine, the empty floor was a grid of lurid squares that matched the colours on the dial.

I jumped back from the window as a speaker set into the corner hissed for my attention. Then the Doctor's voice filled the space, echoing from the tiles like the voice of God.

'Sit on the stool, please, Cassie.'

I found a white stool under the console and her voice continued, brittle as ice. 'One of the reasons people suffer nightmares is repressed violence. In everyday dreams the mind allows man's subconscious to carry out actions that are against his conscious will. For example, I am sure you can imagine a hen-pecked husband who dreams of killing his wife.' There was a pause during which the speaker grille simply hummed and I tried to get my head round what she was saying.

'In your case however it isn't *repressed* violence that's the problem, but *remembered* violence. Your mind is recycling your worst past-life memories.' I nodded to show my understanding, certain the Doctor was watching me. She carried on. 'I believe you experience these *memories* as *nightmares* because society allows you no other outlet for the rage and guilt of your subconscious. And, because you are unable to deal with the feelings your past lives evoke, you repress them and the nightmares become worse. It's a vicious circle. The idea of this study is to see whether acting out a certain level of violence in real life will mean that you do not then need to do so in your dreams.'

I shifted uncomfortably. 'What do you want me to do?' I couldn't see anything dangerous in the room, just the dial and the switch.

'In a moment, one of your peers will enter the other room. He believes I am exploring psychic abilities among your group. Each time you hear the bell you are to turn the dial in front of you to a different colour. He will then choose a square to stand on. If he gets the colour wrong, you are to administer a mild electric shock by throwing the switch.'

My eyes flicked from the dial to the switch to the window.

'The window you are looking through appears to be a mirror on the other side. There is no way for the subject to know who is throwing the switch. He can neither see, nor hear you.'

I imagined giving electric shocks to one of my new friends.

Seth's face floated in front of mine. 'I don't want to hurt anyone.'

The speaker sizzled as if angry. 'We can stop whenever you want, Cassie, but just remember this may help you and your friends.'

I touched the dial.

I have to get rid of my nightmares. And, anyway, I can stop at any time.

The door to the other room opened and Lenny walked in. My heart rose; I almost relished the idea of giving *him* a few mild electric shocks. His feet were bare. I cracked my knuckles in anticipation.

'Let us begin,' the Doctor said.

The bell rang.

Immediately I turned the dial's pointer to yellow and a buzzer sounded in the other room. Lenny looked up with a constipated expression. I almost laughed out loud: he was trying to read my mind. After a moment he stepped on to an orange square.

I reached for the switch then hesitated.

What if this really hurts him?

The speaker hissed into life. 'The research requires that you throw the switch, Cassie.'

Nervously I followed the Doctor's instruction. Lenny hopped as the jolt of electricity reached him. I held my breath until he gave a little shrug, then I exhaled.

It was only a mild shock. He's fine.

The bell sounded and I set the dial to purple. Lenny waited for the buzzer, thought, then moved. As he stepped on to a purple square I sat up straighter.

The bell rang without me having to give a shock. I turned the dial to green. Lenny decided on blue.

I tutted and flicked the switch. This time Lenny yelped and jumped higher.

He was barely given time to step back into the square before the bell sounded once more. I chose pink; Lenny chose yellow.

This time, when I flicked the switch, he danced on the spot. Leaning closer to the window I thought I could see tears in his eyes. These shocks were definitely getting stronger. But before I could be certain he was alright, the bell rang again.

I turned the dial more slowly. Something inside me had shifted and now I willed Lenny to choose the right colour. As I settled on red I watched him anxiously. His foot waved in mid-air. His fists clenched and his mouth worked as if he was chewing gum. With a sinking heart I watched him choose purple.

'Dammit.' My hand inched towards the switch, delaying as long as possible.

The Doctor's voice shattered the quiet. 'The research requires that you continue.'

With a groan I moved the toggle and this time Lenny leaped towards the ceiling. 'That's not fair,' he snivelled. 'I don't want to do this any more.'

The speaker hung silent and unresponsive.

The bell rang.

'Wait a minute. You said we could stop at any time.' I swivelled on my stool, but there was no one to confront.

After a long minute the grille sputtered into life. 'I said *you* could stop at any time.' I opened my mouth, but the Doctor continued. 'Remember how important this is.'

I closed my mouth.

Lenny's a wimp, remember? The shocks probably aren't that bad.

The bell rang, I turned the dial to yellow, but Lenny refused to move.

I blinked at the speaker. 'Now what?'

'He has chosen green.'

'But . . . he didn't move.'

'Not moving still represents a choice. He has chosen green. The research requires that you continue.'

Lenny's arms were crossed, the image of stubborn resolve, and his face showed a tiny smirk. He thought he'd won. My jaw jutted.

You're so annoying, Lenny.

Mechanically I moved the switch. Lenny's back arched and he threw himself off the square with a cry. I winced as he landed and fell on to his side.

The bell rang.

Lenny rose jerkily as if his arms and legs weren't quite under his control. 'I said I'd had enough,' he cried. 'This isn't fun any more.' He made for the door and pounded on the woodwork.

'The subject has selected purple.'

My eyes went to Lenny's feet; the square by the door was purple. His feet were on the square. I swallowed.

'The research requires that you continue.'

I shook my head. 'No – that's enough.'

The speaker was silent for so long I started to wonder if it was broken. In the other room, Lenny shuffled his feet and looked around.

Suddenly his door swung open. For a moment he hung back anxiously as if he expected it to close on him. Then he sprinted for the exit.

'Lie on the bed, Cassie.'

A shelf slid out from the wall. Robotically, I rose from the stool, sat on the bed and lay back. Tears of self-loathing soaked into my hair.

Once my arms were settled at my sides, two nurses entered the room. One pushed a monitor on a trolley. They attached a series of little sticky pads to my chest and forehead. As they worked I stared at the white expanse above me.

What must they think of me?

After an interminable space the nurses left and the Doctor's voice drifted through the speaker. 'Time to sleep.' The lights went out.

* * *

I ache all over. I feel as if I've been kicked by a horse. There is blood on the sheets and heavy drops still add to the pool that is spreading from the bed like gravy.

Hair is glued to my face and neck. I pull it free with a gasp of effort and tuck it behind my neck, utterly exhausted. I've been in labour for two days.

There is a window next to my bed. Evening colours spill into the room and bring the sound of the farm workers heading home for the night. I lay my head on the pillow, fighting sleep even more desperately than usual.

Finally the door opens and he bursts in, carrying our son in his arms, the midwife fussing behind him.

'Dean says congratulations, so do all the men.'

I reach up and he hands our baby back to me. I gaze into his tiny wrinkled face, no bigger than my palm, and eyes dark as midnight stare back into mine.

As I awoke the lights came up and the door opened. The Doctor entered the room with eyebrows raised. 'Well?'

My lungs were so full of tears I could hardly speak. My chest was bloated with the memory of fierce, possessive pride and unbelievable joy.

It was the first time I could remember that I had dreamed of life and not death.

I wasn't hungry so I skipped lunch and considered going straight upstairs to lie down, but I had another treatment in an hour so instead I headed for the TV room, almost floating with happiness.

This is going to work. I could be cured.

But in the TV room I found Lenny in front of the big screen. Shame lodged in my throat and my elation vanished.

He was curled up in the chair staring at the screen. A packet of Monster Munch was open on his knee, but although I watched him for at least two minutes he ate nothing. The room smelled of pickled onion and B.O.

He doesn't know it was me electrocuting him. If he asks, I can say I was in therapy all afternoon.

I started to back away but the boy turned his head. Our eyes locked. Caught, I flushed and gave myself away.

'It was you!' Lenny pointed accusingly then he snatched his arm back as if afraid I'd grab it.

'I'm really sorry.'

'Huh.' His deep-set eyes were red-rimmed.

'I don't know what happened. It got out of control.'

He hunched in the chair as if to make a smaller target of himself.

'I'm not going to hurt you.' I lurched forward and he flinched. 'Stop it, Lenny. Get a grip.'

He scowled. 'Leave me alone.'

Irritation prodded me provokingly to his side. 'It wasn't my fault. It was the *Doctor's* research and you volunteered for it, same as me.'

'I didn't know what it would be like.'

'Well, neither did I.' I glared. 'It couldn't have been that bad. You look fine.'

Mama's boy. The thought blew through my head and the room spun. I clenched my fists, maddened and a little afraid. 'You'd have done the same if our roles had been reversed.'

'I wouldn't.'

Liar. 'If I'd been in that room, you'd have let it go on longer.'

Elsewhere in the Manor a door slammed and we both stopped.

I realised that I was towering over the boy, as intimidating as the Doctor. I swallowed and retreated. 'I'm sure the Doctor wouldn't have taken it any further. She wouldn't have let you come to any harm.'

As I spoke, however, I remembered that none of the staff had gone to help Lenny off the diving board . . . and couldn't help wondering how much further she would have let me go.

CHAPTER FOURTEEN
SECRET

I headed into the rec room, trying to hold on to the memory of my last dream, but Lenny had made me so angry I could hardly see. Walking as if I was made of china I made my way to the window seat and traced the initials I had carved into the sill.

Abruptly, long legs stretched out next to mine. 'Nice one,' Pandra jerked her head towards my defacement of the stone. 'The Doctor should've been spewing, but she says it's a sign of your progress.'

I answered her with a mouth that felt stuffed with cotton wool. 'It can't be . . . I don't even remember doing it.'

Pandra nudged my hand aside and traced the lettering with a ringed finger. 'Your strongest past life is coming out.'

Trying to shake the fuzzy feeling out of my head I faced her. 'Do you do stuff you can't remember?'

'Sometimes.' Pandra fiddled with her eyebrow stud. 'Not as

often now. The Doctor says it's because I'm learning to accept who I am.'

'Who's that?'

She shrugged. 'If normal people are made up of their experiences, then we're the sum of all our past lives . . . That's what the Doctor says.'

I cocked my head, interested. 'So who are you a sum of?'

'You want names?' Pandra shifted on her seat and the dragon on her necklace slipped out of her T-shirt.

I stared at the necklace then shook my head. 'It wouldn't mean anything to me anyway.' I leaned against the glass. Condensation darkened my top, but I didn't move, grateful for the cool. 'Lenny's a festering boil, isn't he?' I didn't mean to say it out loud; the words just jumped out.

Pandra nodded, grim faced. 'He's weak, a pathetic runt and an insult to humanity, but there's nothing we can do about it. Just ignore him. I do.' I stared at her and she looked at me, calculating. 'Did you know Seth's a Catholic?' When I didn't react she pulled back. 'It doesn't bother you . . .'

'That he's a Catholic? Course not.' I frowned and rubbed the back of my neck. It still ached from the night before. 'Is that why you don't like him? You don't like *Catholics*?'

'I don't like any of them.' She spat the words and her pretty blue eyes flashed. 'They're all weak.'

Suddenly chilled I examined her face for a sign that she was joking. 'Have you always felt this way?' Her eyes flickered and I thought I had my answer. 'Just since you came here . . .'

She slid backwards. 'It's just the way I feel. All our feelings are valid and should be acted on. Just because I've been repressing stuff because of societal norms . . .'

'I bet that's what the Doctor says too.'

Pandra caught my wrist in a death grip, as if she was drowning and wanted to take me down with her. 'To become all we can be and meet our destinies, we have to accept who we are.' She looked around, eyes narrowed furtively. 'Come on, I want to show you something.' She hauled me to my feet.

For the first time since I'd arrived at the Manor I was heading for the exterior door so I let Pandra drag me along and waited as she swiped her key card through the slot. As she slipped it back in her pocket it struck me that the cards were a neat way of tracking us.

Is someone watching us right now?

* * *

By the time we reached the treeline my Converse had soaked through and I stepped off the wet grass gratefully. Then I looked around, abruptly nervous. 'Is the wood part of the grounds?'

'Sure. Sounds like the Doctor gave you the speech about flash floods. You don't need to worry if you're with me. I've been here ages . . . I know what I'm doing.' Pandra set off.

I glanced back across the lawn then I took a deep breath and followed.

The first trees we passed were birch, but as we walked the ranks of slender, silver trunks gave way to thicker, more twisted species. Ones I mostly didn't recognise. The light took on an emerald quality as it filtered through a blanket of leaves and I shivered as we picked our way over misshapen roots. 'Um . . . should we be this far from the Manor?'

Pandra shrugged. 'The Doctor doesn't mind. She knows I need a special place away from the others . . . I don't mind sharing it with *you*, though.' She beamed at me as she lifted a branch out of her path. Her face was half shadowed by a twisted oak. With her cropped hair and pierced ears she looked like a deranged nymph. 'Be careful here, it's slippery.' She disappeared.

I leaped forward and saw her picking her way down a rocky slope that led into a narrow gorge.

My vision blurred. I could easily imagine the roar of white water as it boiled along the bottom.

If there is a flood, we'll be swept away.

I swallowed. Thorny bushes dotted the hillside. They looked like twists of barbed wire.

In fact it looked just like the dream I'd had in my very first therapy session.

The world spun and I swayed.

'Come on,' Pandra shouted.

I held my fists underneath my chin. 'I-I can't.'

Pandra stopped, looked at me then, with a shake of her head, made her way back up. 'I'll help you down. You really want to see this.'

'I don't think . . .' Pandra grabbed my right wrist and yanked me off balance. Before I could catch myself I was on to the scree. 'W-wait,' I gasped, but Pandra ignored me.

'You have to face your fears. Whatever the dream is, next time it'll be easier because you've done this. Believe me.'

My foot slid into a patch of bramble. Thorns stole into the gap between my trainers and jeans and jabbed my ankle. I screamed as if I'd been stabbed.

Pandra clapped her hand over my mouth. 'This is my *secret* place, remember?'

Waves of terror bore me to my knees. Pandra came down with me, her hand still over my mouth. Distantly I heard my breath whistling through my nose. My vision blurred, I couldn't see and the rustling of the leaves overhead sounded like rain.

Volleys of rain hammer my back. I whimper through chattering teeth and even that small movement works the wire barbs further in.

I try to wriggle free of the post that pins me. I only have to move a few inches to escape the water but I can't force my body to obey.

'Stop it. You'll make us fall off the edge.' Pandra's hand was still covering my face and her rings dug into my nose and chin. Her other arm was crooked round my shoulder and she had her legs wrapped round me.

I heaved, trying to shift her, but she held on. 'Cassie!' she wailed.

I froze. I had been taken over by a dream, but I certainly hadn't fallen asleep on this hillside.

Hysterical laughter bubbled up and I clutched at Pandra with desperation strengthening my fingers. She held on to me until she felt me start to relax then released her hand from my mouth. 'Okay?'

Struggling for breath I shook my head and yanked my foot from the tangle of thorns. My heart raced, but I was starting to feel like myself.

I am Cassiopeia Farrier. I'm on a hill near Mount Hermon. There's no barbed wire. There's no flood. It's not raining.

Eventually my lungs opened and I started to breathe more easily. I slumped full length to the ground and ignored the stones that jabbed at me through my shirt.

Pandra slid away from me on her rump. 'You were speaking *German.*' Her foot was still tangled with mine but she didn't pull away.

'I-I was?'

'Damn.' She sounded almost as shaken as me. 'One of your other selves is dead close to the surface. The Doctor's going to be well happy.'

'Happy!' I scrambled to my feet.

Am I going to have nightmares while I'm awake now? I-I'll go insane.

Pandra caught my elbow as I started to shake. 'It isn't far now. I'll help you to the bottom of the hill.'

I focused on the ground beneath my feet rather than think about what I was doing. Rotting leaves covered loose stones and I skidded a couple of times, but Pandra caught me and I muttered thanks as I fixed my gaze on the scurrying beetles disturbed by my clumsy descent.

Suddenly Pandra let go of my arm. 'There, you did it.'

I glanced back. The slope towered behind me, ragged as an old man's throat. Quickly I looked for the path Pandra intended us to take.

A dry stream bed wound towards sheer rock. Pandra set off along it and I followed, casting nervous glances back at the treeline.

In front of the rock wall there was a bush. Pandra stopped. 'Here,' she said proudly, and widened her arms.

'But . . . there's nothing there.'

Pandra grabbed the thorny bush by its leaves and yanked it

aside. It moved easily, its roots barely anchoring it into the pebbles. Behind it, a dark hole gaped like a maw. A smell emerged with the oozing darkness, rank and rotten.

'Oh. You want to go in there?' I whispered, unable to raise my voice.

Pandra giggled. 'There's a torch just inside. Isn't it great?'

Luckily she didn't wait for my answer, but ducked into the darkness. My hand twitched as if to pull her back, but she was gone before I could reach the tail of her shirt.

Suddenly a beam of light clicked on and she peered out of the gloom. 'Follow me.' She turned back into the cave and let the light play over the rocks inside.

I bent almost double and followed her across the threshold.

A few feet in, the cave opened to head height and I found Pandra on a rug by the back wall. 'Here.' She moved the torch to the floor. I saw that I was about to step on to rotting wooden boards. I skirted round them and she shuffled sideways to give me room. Gingerly I sat on the blanket next to her, trying to squash the spiders and other creeping things that scuttled into my imagination.

Through the remaining leaves of the bush a little light filtered from the world outside and my eyes started to adjust. Pandra held the torch loosely in her left hand. With her right she felt under the rug. 'Want one?' She held out a can of Coke.

'Where'd you get these?'

'Swiped 'em from the kitchen. I've got some food here too, 'cause we'll probably miss tea.' She popped her can and took a large gulp. Then she smacked her lips. 'Sweet, sweet caffeine.'

The smell in the cave was too strong for me to even consider drinking. Without being too conspicuous I tried to cover my mouth with my sleeve.

'Great, isn't it? All the comforts of home. Well, some of my homes anyway. I don't know about yours . . .' Pandra stretched. 'The best bit is no one knows we're here.'

Suspicion tickled my neck. 'Not even the Doctor?'

Pandra smirked. 'She knows I have a place, but not exactly where. She says a bit of privacy is good for my treatment.'

I rocked my head towards her. 'Do you really think the Doctor's helped you?'

The torchlight wavered towards my face. I held my arm up to ward off the beam and Pandra's voice emerged from the shadows. 'Don't you?'

'I feel worse than I did before.' I fumbled for the right words. 'I feel like I'm . . . unravelling. I'm having nightmares while I'm awake. I'm thinking in German but I can't remember the name of my German teacher. I can hum Lohengrin for you if you want.' I paused. 'I've never even *heard* Lohengrin, but Zillah must have . . .' My voice rose to an odd high pitch and I clamped my lips together, certain Pandra wouldn't be impressed with hysterics.

Something cold touched my wrist and I gasped, ready to knock the creature off, but it was Pandra. 'It'll all be alright. She says it's like being born. There's a painful bit, but then you'll accept who you are.'

'I want to be Cassie Farrier. Not Zillah. Not some other dead person. They've lived their lives. I want this one.'

There was such a long silence that I wondered whether Pandra was going to respond.

Finally her voice shivered in the dead air. 'You're like me, I can tell.'

'What do you mean?'

'I have something that'll help.'

The light sliced round the cave, then stilled as she balanced the torch on a ledge.

Pandra bent over the rough boards that lay in front of the rug, removing them one by one.

'Look.' She caught my shoulder and pulled me forward. Off balance I landed with my hands by the edge of the last plank. Next to me I could sense, rather than see, a gaping hole.

'What is it?' I gagged, the smell I had noticed before now filled the already dank cave. 'Pandra . . . that smell.'

Her head cocked towards me, half into the shaft of cold torch-light. She seemed completely unfazed. 'You'll get used to it.' She picked up the torch and focused it for me on the top of the hole.

A few feet down a lumpy ledge extended about a third of the way across the opening. Underneath a deeper darkness sucked at my gaze. I started to topple.

Pandra steadied me. 'Careful.' Her face leered into mine. 'I'm not sure how deep that is.'

'You found this?'

Pandra nodded and moved the torch so the dusty beam played over the ledge.

Oh, my God . . . it's covered in dead animals.

My back smacked into rock with bruising force. I hadn't realised I had scrambled so fast from the hole, but my feet still made pointless cycling motions on the rug as if I could burrow further back. 'Is this some sort of pet cemetery? Why are you showing me this? I almost fell in there . . .'

My chest rose and fell in small pants. I was living a nightmare: each time I breathed, I sucked in air that was poisoned with death and rot. I retched and covered my mouth.

On some of the dead creatures maggots had moved like a wriggling blanket. Now, agitated flies buzzed around me and I pictured them feasting on the sightless eyes.

Pandra was watching me, cross-legged and calm. 'Cool, isn't it,' she said.

'C-cool?' Bile rose to my throat.

'There's thirty in there.'

'Thirty . . . dead animals?' I heaved, not caring if I hurt her feelings.

Light caught her chin; it flayed her face and turned it into a skull. 'They're not all large ones. I started small, but I caught a hare last week, – it was even bigger than the terrier.' Enthusiasm lit her more clearly than the torchlight.

I thought I must have misunderstood her but she continued, happy to be sharing her secret.

'Yeah, I've got all this knowledge about traps. Soon you'll be able to access yours about weapons. It's the same sort of thing.' Cheerfully she tapped her forehead with a single finger. 'I've got them all over this wood, though, so if you want to come here it's best you come with me – don't come alone.'

'Traps?' I mouthed.

'How do you think I caught a hare, silly? It's not like I outran it.' She giggled, and it was such a normal sound that my belly tightened. 'It's amazing. It's so . . . cathartic.' Pandra took a deep breath, inhaling the tainted air as if it was a seaside breeze. 'I have this amazing power. I can kill something quick, or slow. I can make it suffer, let it die easy, or even let it go.'

I tried to back away from her, but her grip on my arm was unwavering. She was stronger than I was, much stronger.

'You'll love it, Cassie. All my life I've felt out of control. I've been bounced around homes. I know Seth told you.' She glowered. 'But it isn't just that, it's the dreams. I can't control what I see, how it makes me feel. I still can't, despite all my time here. All my life, waking, sleeping, I've felt like I've been on someone else's joyride. You know?'

My head dropped automatically. I did know.

'This gives you power. You become like God.' She paused. 'You did one of the Doctor's experiments today, so I know you can see how this could help you.'

'But . . . you're still having the dreams. You said so.'

'I've got more control now. Sometimes I can stop them, make myself wake up. And sometimes I see other stuff too, not just death and violence.'

Instantly my thoughts went to the dream I'd had earlier that day and the joy it had filled me with. As if she could sense my wavering heart Pandra rattled my elbow. 'There's a part of you that wants this. I can see it. We're the same.'

I shook my head. 'We're not,' I whispered, and pulled my arm away. 'I'd never do this.'

'Never?' Pandra licked her lips. 'Maybe I showed you too soon.' She pouted. 'The Doctor said your progress was incredible. I thought maybe you were ready.' She sagged like a disappointed child. 'I should've waited.'

'The Doctor knows about this?'

Enigmatically Pandra smiled and I scuttled crab-like towards the cave entrance.

'At least help me put the boards back,' Pandra called, and her voice grew cross.

My hands found the bush and as I shoved it away from the exit, bright daylight jabbed into my eyes. I half rolled on to the stream bed, wheezing and clutching my stomach. I badly wanted to see Seth.

'You won't tell the others, will you?' Her voice floated anxiously after me. 'This is my secret place.'

Chapter Fifteen
DECISION

I pelted up the stairs and barely hesitated before turning towards Seth's room. I didn't even consider that he might not be there and indeed the door opened immediately in response to my pounding fist.

Seth was wearing his pyjamas. He blinked slowly at the sight of me. 'What's the matter, Cass?'

I tried to speak, but couldn't squeeze the words out.

Seth stepped aside and reached for my arm. 'Come on in, the bell isn't due for a while.'

I focused on his outfit and the hint of toothpaste at the corner of his mouth. 'Y-you were going to bed?' My voice sounded strained even to me.

'I was getting an early night, but I'd rather see you.' He pulled me inside and nudged the door closed with his foot. 'Here.' He guided me to his bed then knelt in front of me and took my hands. 'You're freezing.' He rubbed them vigorously. 'You look awful, what happened?'

I wouldn't let myself cry. I curled my toes and tried to force some iron into my spine. I'd come here without thinking, an automatic reaction to the darkness Pandra had shown me.

Should I tell him about her secret place?

I hung my head as I wondered what to say.

If the Doctor already knows, telling Seth would just upset him.

I gulped back a lump in my throat. 'I'm drowning,' I whispered truthfully.

His hands stopped rubbing mine for a moment. 'What do you mean?'

My shoulders were touching my earlobes, I was so tense. 'I've started having dreams while I'm awake. Like . . . visions, you know? I remember music I've never heard. I h-hate Lenny.' I swallowed. 'I mean I really hate him and there's no reason for it. I can't remember things like . . . my mother's maiden name . . . but I've got all this extra stuff in my head. I know how to clean a bolt action rifle . . .'

I realised I was getting hysterical and tried to clamp down my emotions, but exhaustion made it impossible. I had to pull my hands back so that I could dig the heels of my palms into my eyes. 'I nearly hurt Pandra earlier. I couldn't help myself. I wasn't even in control of my body . . . and next week the firing range will be finished and I'll have to start *shooting!*'

'It's alright.' Seth tried to take my hands away from my face, but I wouldn't let him. He stood. 'I'm going to get you a drink of water.'

I leaped on the chance to compose myself and stole several deep breaths. Seth returned with a drink and put it in my hand. I focused on the glass and lowered my voice, conscious that we might be overheard. 'Do *you* think the Doctor's helping us?'

After a long silence I had to look up. Seth's lips were white. Finally he replied, just as quietly, 'I don't know. But we can't risk leaving. What if we're supposed to feel like this just before some sort of breakthrough?'

I nodded grimly. 'The Doctor asked me to take part in one of her research projects.'

Seth straightened. 'Tell her no! That research has totally screwed Pandra up.'

My breath came heavier.

It's okay for him; he obviously doesn't need the money.

'Oh, Cass.' My name emerged on a sigh. 'You said yes?'

My knees shook and I pressed them together. 'She says if we're violent in real life we'll have less violent dreams . . . maybe even be free of them altogether.'

He sat next to me. 'What did she make you do?'

I spoke to the floor. 'I-I electrocuted Lenny.'

'You did what?' I glanced up and Seth's eyes glinted. 'Is he alright?'

'I th-think so.'

Seth paused for a moment, staring at me. Then when he spoke his voice had gone quiet. 'Would you believe I was once like him – Lenny?'

I shook my head and tried not to stare too obviously at the muscles beneath his lightweight pyjamas.

'I was a little kid and badly bullied.' He clenched his fists. 'Mum tried to stop it but when she spoke to the school it got worse. Dad didn't want to know what was happening. He thought I should learn to stand up for myself. He's not interested in whining.'

'Oh.' My heart ached for him.

If I feel this bad for Seth, why can't I feel sorry for Lenny?

He gestured at his scarred neck. 'This happened on my eleventh birthday. I wanted a trip to the cinema, but Dad booked an assault course. He invited every boy in my class. All day I was shoved off platforms and dumped in the mud while he watched.'

'. . . And didn't do anything?'

Seth shook his head. 'At the end of the day a few of the bigger guys ganged up on me and I finally fought back. Stupidly I picked the highest platform to make my stand. When they pushed me off I landed on a tree branch.' He smiled bleakly. 'Dad said he'd follow the ambulance, but there was some sort of emergency at work. He didn't come to the hospital until the next day.'

'W-what happened to the boys that did this?'

Seth's eyes focused back on the present. 'Nothing.' He looked surprised at my question. 'I didn't moan about it, I got better and they never touched me again. I guess they realised it had all gone too far. Dad suggested I start working out. That must've helped too.'

'Oh.' Suddenly cold I wrapped my arms round myself. 'Your past life . . . the one you wouldn't talk about. It reminds you of your birthday . . . makes you feel like a victim.'

Seth nodded.

'I still feel awful about what I did to Lenny.'

'I'll check on him before bed.' Seth paused. 'You won't do it again, will you?'

'Electrocute him?'

'The Doctor's extra-curricular experiments.'

I shook my head. 'I-I don't know.' He opened his mouth but I didn't let him speak. 'It worked.'

'You had a *good dream*?' He forgot to whisper.

I clutched his hand. 'I'd just given birth. It hurt as much as any of my deaths, so that part wasn't good. But . . . I got to hold this baby in my arms and I knew he was mine. Seth, I'd done this incredible thing, I'd *made* him. I woke up with this feeling of . . . just amazing joy.'

'I don't believe it.' His shoulders sagged. 'But we can't hurt other people just to get rid of our nightmares.'

'I . . . I guess not,' I replied.

Seth sighed wistfully. 'You know, the only time I don't dream about death is when I dream about this book and *that's* almost the worst nightmare of the lot.'

My head shot up. 'You dream about a book? D-does it have a black cover?'

I'd thought Seth's face was pale before, but now his scar stood out against his neck livid as a fresh wound. He gripped my shoulders. 'You've seen it too?'

Slowly I nodded. 'How is that possible?'

'I-it isn't just the book I dreamed about.' Seth's fingers contracted slightly and his eyes towed mine to his sculptures, which now stood exposed in the corner of the room.

I looked at the carvings, not understanding. 'What?'

'You still don't recognise yourself?' His voice was hoarse.

I laughed nervously. 'That's not me.' The statue was beautiful, all flowing hair, graceful limbs and slanted eyes that drew me in like lodes. 'I don't look like that.'

Surprise evertook Seth's expression. 'You do to me.'

I hesitated. 'Did the Doctor see this before I got here?'

He nodded. 'It was the first thing I made. It's been here for weeks.'

'So . . . when I went to see her in London, she'd seen this already.' I frowned, but I couldn't work out if it meant anything.

Maybe the Doctor didn't even recognise me from Seth's sculpture.

Seth's mismatched eyes darkened. 'She probably thought it would freak you out if she mentioned that one of her other patients had made a statue of you.' He cleared his throat and let me go. The sudden absence of his hands made me shiver.

Regardless of the Doctor's motives I had my own confession

to make. 'I-I dreamed of you too,' I whispered.

Seth's fingers hovered over my left hand. 'I did wonder.'

'But *how*?' I focused on his swollen knuckle rather than look at his face.

'Perhaps we've met in a past life.'

I half turned and gestured at the sculpture. 'That doesn't explain how you knew what I'd look like in this life.' I thought of Zillah. 'I looked different last time.'

Seth hummed thoughtfully and his breath caressed my mouth. My tongue flicked across my bottom lip; I tasted toothpaste and raised my eyes.

He was staring at me; my reflection shone in the growing blackness of his pupils. His fingers caught mine and unthinkingly I moved my right palm on to his thigh. Through the cotton of his pyjamas his bunched muscles felt hot as brands.

The sound of a ringing bell exploded into the room and I gave a small shriek. Seth jolted, a flush bruised his face and guiltily he jumped back.

'We *can't*.' His voice was so hoarse it was barely recognisable. 'It's a rule here.'

Humiliation fried me to my toes. 'I know.' I moved until there was a wide gap between us. 'I should go to my room.' Seth nodded, but I didn't leave.

I had to tell him all I knew. I cleared my throat. 'Seth . . . you know the book?'

His eyes narrowed in acknowledgement.

'I've seen it. I-it belongs to the Doctor.'

For a moment Seth displayed no reaction then small muscles tensed in his jaw. 'Are you sure?'

'I saw her reading it on my first day here.' Seth swore under his breath and I continued talking in an undertone. 'I-I don't trust the Doctor. There's something going on here and I'm sure that book has something to do with it.'

Seth nodded grimly. 'Then we have to get a look at it.'

'The Doctor went nuts when I saw her with it. She won't just show it to us.'

He clenched his fists. 'If only there was a way we could search her office . . .'

'But we're not allowed to leave our rooms after the final bell.' Frustration pushed my words through gritted teeth. 'This place is like a prison!'

'We can't even sneak out.' Seth gestured towards the barred

window and his face caught the light.

A noise at his door made us spin as if we were on a spit. The lock snicked, the handle turned and it swung open. The Doctor stood in the frame, filling the corridor.

Lenny grinned evilly from behind her. 'Told you she'd be in here,' he said.

A swift count of the dead tells me two are missing.

I frown, rest my gun on my shoulder and turn slowly. My heel grinds on broken glass and I look down. There's a satchel under my boot. A broken picture of a smiling woman is crushed under it. I kick it aside.

Which way did they run? With barley this high, they could be hiding anywhere. I step forward. Hans calls to me, but I wave him back. I need quiet.

Off to my right the barley seems more damaged than it should be and a smear of blood on one of the leaves is more than just spatter.

They went that way . . . but there's nowhere for them to go. The nearest building is the castle in the distance. I hum a little under my breath as I follow their trail.

* * *

Next morning I could barely drag myself down to breakfast. Apart from the fact that the idea of seeing Pandra again was making my belly ache, horrifying dreams had ramped through my head during the night as if the day's experiment had never happened.

After waking from another new nightmare I'd spent my time trying to think of a way to get into the Doctor's office without being caught.

There's an obvious solution, Cassiopeia. Call your parents and just get the hell out of here.

I ducked into the lobby payphone then stopped, holding my key card. I needed it to activate the phone, so the Doctor would know I was making the call.

I'll just have to be careful.

'Mum, I can't stay here any more.' There was silence on the other end and I clutched the receiver tighter.

Have we been cut off?

'Mum?'

'I'm here.' She sounded resigned. 'Let me get your dad.'

My leg jiggled as I waited.

Soon Dad'll be on his way to pick me up. Tonight I'll be sleeping in my own bed.

I leaned wearily on the wall. Every muscle screamed, my head ached abominably and my eyes were sore from crying. I so badly wanted some rest.

'Cassie?' It was Dad.

'I can't stay here, Dad. Please come and get me.'

'Cassie, I really did hope not to get this call.'

I turned my face further into the wall. 'I know, but it's bad here. I-I can't explain on the phone, but you have to come.'

'It's barely been a fortnight. Have you given the treatment a chance?'

Panic started to raise my voice. 'You don't understand, I'm getting worse, not better, there're things going on here . . . I can't tell you right now.'

I heard Dad tap the receiver. 'The thing is, honey . . .' He paused and a black hole started to open in my heart. 'The thing is, when we sent you there we had to sign a document.'

My voice sounded tinny. 'What kind of document?'

There was another long pause. 'Doctor Ashworth is your legal guardian for the duration of your treatment. You can't leave until she agrees you're ready. We'll speak to her, call her now; maybe she'll agree to release you early. Call us back in an hour and I'll let you know what she says.'

I dropped the receiver back on to the cradle and leaned against the wall of the booth, too numb even to cry. There was no way the Doctor was going to agree to my departure, not with the 'excellent progress' I was making. I was trapped.

'Doctor Ashworth says it's completely normal.' Dad answered the phone immediately when I called back. 'Paranoia is one of the symptoms of sleep deprivation and you're in a strange place surrounded by strange people.' His voice dropped. 'You have to try harder. We didn't want to tell you this, but we had to remortgage the house so you could go to Mount Hermon. You need to listen to the Doctor and get better. Everything will be fine. You just have to be brave and get over this adjustment period, okay?'

Dragging my feet I headed into the dining room. Then I stopped. Lenny was on his way out. Seeing me, his eyes widened and he looked for another way to go.

I felt dizzy again and dug my fists into my eyes, trying to make the room stay still. When I looked back up, Lenny had disappeared and the kitchen door was swinging shut.

Wearily I scanned the tables. There was a spare seat next to Lizzie and I made for it, ignoring Pandra's welcoming fork wave.

I dropped into the seat and I looked at my hands. They shook all the time now, as if I had palsy.

I have to find that book. If it proves I'm getting worse, then Dad'll have to get me out of here.

I reached blindly for a slice of toast.

But if the Doctor catches me she'll call the police. I'll be done for breaking and entering . . . and the German authorities are probably still looking for me.

I lowered the toast before I could crush it into crumbs and my thoughts raced like rats in a maze as I tried to think of a way to get out of my room without being caught.

The barred windows meant I had to use the door. But the key card was the only way to open it and that would bring someone looking.

I have to fool the key-card system . . .

Lizzie was watching me with an odd expression; I'd been holding the same piece of toast in the air for several minutes.

Quickly I bit off a mouthful and chewed contemplatively. Each time I'd used my card to open a door a light above the slot had changed from red to green. So there had to be a sensor in the door frame.

I was chewing my cheek, my toast long disintegrated. I took another absent-minded bite from the piece in my hand.

If I put something inside the door frame . . . can I fool the sensor into thinking my door is locked when it isn't?

I sat up straighter.

'Lizzie?' I addressed the younger girl in a half whisper.

'Mmm?' She swallowed a mouthful of Frosties but waved her spoon to show she was listening.

'Could you make some little wooden rectangles for me?'

Lizzie gave a half shrug, half nod.

'How long would it take?'

Her spoon knocked on her bowl. 'You want them carved or anything?'

I shook my head.

'A few minutes each. Not long. What're they for?'

Inspiration struck me. 'I've got an idea for Double Dares.'

Lizzie grinned. 'Cool.' She leaned forward. 'Are you going to let me in on it? Double Dares is my game you know.'

I wrinkled my nose. 'I need to test it first. Is that okay?'

She flounced back in her chair. 'I suppose so.'

I fiddled with the toast on my plate and stared. Lizzie was usually in constant motion, her curls bouncing, her face animated. It wasn't often I saw her still, but for a moment the small disappointment revealed a different girl: overweight and spotty with frizzy hair. Somehow her usual gyroscopic movement disguised all that.

I frowned. 'Lizzie, how'd you get into Double Dares anyway?'

She blinked. 'I just did, I guess.' She looked away for a moment then turned back. 'After some nights I could just curl up in a corner and never show my face. You know what I mean?'

I nodded.

'Double Dares keeps me *doing* stuff. It reminds me not to just give in to all this.' She swallowed. 'Otherwise I'm just a walking dishrag: the clean-up after some dead guy's power trip. If I keep taking risks, like with Double Dares, then I'm living my life.'

I cleared my throat. 'If I get you some measurements, do you think you could do those wooden blocks for me today?'

Lizzie picked up Nutella-smeared toast, hesitated, then bit.

'No problem.' She nodded and butter dripped down her chin.

After breakfast I returned to my room. I pretended to re-tie my trainers in the doorway and examined the lock. There was a bump inside that might, or might not, be the sensor I'd imagined.

Mum had left me a sewing kit. I found the tape measure then made sure I was alone and measured the gap in the doorframe. After scribbling the figures on to the back of a bit of thread-wrapped card I ran to the art room.

I handed the card to Lizzie. 'Here're the measurements. Could you put a groove in the top of each one, so they can be lifted out easily?'

'No problem.' Lizzie glanced at the card and dropped it carelessly on her workbench.

'Lizzie, could you keep this secret?'

'Obviously.' She slid her goggles over her eyes.

Meaningfully I tilted my head towards the card. She snorted and slipped it into her pocket. 'Paranoid much?'

I shuffled my feet. 'This place is enough to make anyone paranoid.'

'Yeah.' Lizzie glanced at the woodshop door then rotated her shoulders as if to shrug off some discomfort. 'How many of these do you want?'

'Four would be great, thanks.'

'Come back in half an hour.' She picked up a block of wood and prepared to cut.

Forty minutes later I was back in my room with the little wooden pieces.

When I was sure the corridor was empty I slipped one into my doorframe, thankful that the only security cameras I'd found in the Manor were in the recreational areas. My hands were shaking so much that I almost dropped it, but it fitted perfectly. I held my breath, stepped into the hall and let the door swing closed.

Anxiously I looked at the little light. It was red. The door wasn't locked, but the system believed it was. I muffled a whoop and put my palm to the door.

Now for the real test . . . will it open?

I leaned my weight on it but nothing happened.

'Damn.' I couldn't suppress the impulse to pound on the door and abruptly it gave way. I fell into my room, staggered, caught myself and did a little jig of delight.

I found a way to get around without my key card.

I stared at the wooden pieces scattered on my bedspread. I only hoped the other doors in the Manor worked the same way.

I didn't have the final appointment of the day, so I had to come up with a reason for going to see the Doctor last thing.

'My head's splitting, can I have some paracetamol?'

Doctor Ashworth lifted her head from beneath her desk and arched a flawless brow. 'You didn't have to come to me for that. You could have spoken to any of the nurses.' She straightened in her chair. 'Why are you really here?'

I tucked my hands into my sleeves.

I have to tell her something she'll believe. It has to be the truth.

'I'm worried about what's happening to me.'

The Doctor's lips opened like the petals of a carnivorous flower. A tiny thread of spittle remained stuck between them until she licked it away. 'Everything is fine, Cassie. You're responding remarkably well.'

'Pandra said one of my past lives is close to the surface. What does that mean?'

The Doctor leaned into her chair. 'Yes, she told me about the incident yesterday.' She didn't elaborate so I had no idea how much she knew. I also noticed that she didn't answer my question.

My eye twitched. 'Should that be happening?' Finally I voiced my greatest fear. 'I feel like I'm being taken over.'

The Doctor smiled widely. 'That's just silly. It's your brain accommodating a lot of new information.'

'B-but I'm forgetting things from my own life.'

The Doctor shook her head. 'You of all people should know that you never forget anything; it's all there, in your subconscious. Think of your conscious mind as a . . .' She paused. 'As a bath. Your subconscious is the water tank; your memories are the water. You only have so much room in your conscious mind, your bath, as it were.' She smiled at her own cleverness. 'At the moment your brain is making space for the knowledge we're bringing out of your subconscious by letting some of the water out of your bath.'

'My memories are getting flushed away?'

'Well, that's where my analogy breaks down.' The Doctor shrugged her enormous shoulders. 'Imagine that your bath is part of a closed system. Instead of going back out to sea, your own memories are being returned to the water tank for a while. Soon you'll reach a balance. You'll be able to access what you need from the tank of your subconscious memory: knowledge and skills from your past lives, for example, without the bath overflowing.'

I dug my nails into my palms. 'Like being able to put a gun together?'

The Doctor inclined her head. 'Exactly. That's one skill your mind has learned to retrieve by itself.' She stroked her hands over the leather blotter on her desk.

'So . . . this is just an adjustment period?'

'That's right.' She gestured to the door. The interview was over.

I palmed one of the little wooden nuggets. As I left I pretended to stumble on the door jamb and slipped the wood into the gap. I almost moaned with relief when it fitted.

The Doctor looked up sharply. 'Are you alright?'

'I'm fine. Sorry.' I backed into the corridor.

Now I just had to do the same to the door in the hallway. The gap seemed slightly smaller than the others, so I had to jam the little rectangle in, but when I left it seemed to be working. Luckily the only one around to spot my suspicious loitering was Seth.

'What're you doing?'

I pulled out my key card. 'Come outside and I'll tell you.'

* * *

Seth marched next to me, hands in his pockets, but otherwise apparently impervious to the biting wind. His hair, escaped from its band, slashed over his face and his scar almost glowed in the cold air.

I told him about the blockers and for a while after I'd finished speaking he said nothing.

'Seth?'

He continued to stride wordlessly. His gaze was fixed on the new range beyond the tennis courts. It was almost finished.

Finally he stopped walking. 'Do you really want to risk breaking into the Doctor's office?'

I nodded. 'I'm sure she isn't trying to cure us. Pandra's been here over a year and even her dreams aren't gone. I know there's supposed to be an adjustment period, but I can't believe I'm meant to feel this bad.' I held my elbows close to my chest. 'I came here because I thought I was going crazy. I figured I couldn't feel any worse. I was wrong. I-I'm at the point where I'd be grateful just to have my old nightmares back.'

He clenched his fists. 'I know what you mean.'

'Then there's the fact that we both dreamed about each other . . . and the book.'

Seth started walking again. I jogged to catch up with him and snagged my trainers on a chunk of dirt. Seth caught my arm and didn't pull away after I'd caught my balance, so I left my elbow curled around his and pressed the spare door blocker into his other hand. 'You'll need this if you want to help me.'

He dropped it into his pocket. 'I'll come and get you just after midnight.'

'No . . . We should meet in the Doctor's office. If one of us is caught getting there, at least the other might make it.'

He shuffled his feet. 'There's a chance this really is an adjustment period. If we're caught, we'll be sent home.'

'I-I know.' I jammed my toes into the mud. 'Do you still want to do this?'

Seth nodded. 'We might get away with it if we have a good enough cover story. She found you in my room last night.'

'So?'

'If the blockers don't work like you think or we're caught out in the open, couldn't we say we were planning on meeting somewhere? It probably won't work if we're actually found in the Doctor's office, but anywhere else it might get us a pass.'

I stopped walking. 'So if we get caught we let them think we . . .'

He actually blushed. 'They might not send us home if they think we're just horny.'

'My dad would kill me.'

'It's only if we get caught, and I don't plan to.'

I sighed. 'Alright . . . tonight then.'

He nodded seriously. 'Tonight.'

CHAPTER SIXTEEN

BREAK-IN

I waited anxiously as the clock ticked towards twelve. The nurses had finished their rounds long ago and I couldn't wait any longer or nerves would wreck my resolve.

I reached under the pillow for the lump that had helped keep me awake for the last couple of hours. I'd taken Lizzie's chisel. I hoped I wouldn't need it but, at the same time, I wasn't expecting the book to be waiting for us on the desk.

I slid out of bed as silently as I could, stuffed the tool into the elastic of my pyjama bottoms, padded to the door in bare feet and slipped into the corridor.

When the door thudded into place I held my breath.

I don't care what Lizzie says about taking risks. I'm not cut out for this.

I sped along the corridor, crabwise, as quickly and silently as I could.

* * *

I ran headlong until I reached the door marked *Treatment Area*.
With barely a pause I shoved with both hands, as if the Doctor
herself was hunting me. The door opened and I fell through just
as a voice floated round the corner.

'Which room is it?'

They've already found me out . . .

I crouched behind the door. If the blocker hadn't worked, they
knew I was out of my room, but probably not where I was. I pushed
a knuckle into my mouth to muffle my own breathing.

What do I do?

If I waited until they hit the stairs, I could sprint for the rec
room. It would make sense to say I was meeting Seth there, but I
couldn't move.

'It's the youngest boy this time.'

I struggled to understand. Then my thoughts cleared: *The
nurses are going to Lenny's room.*

'It was that ruddy experiment. It's the second time I've been
called up there tonight and it's not even midnight.'

My neck flopped as if the muscles had died and I rested my
forehead on my knees.

They aren't looking for me. At least . . . not yet.

I sat motionless as the voices receded.

When I finally lifted my head the corridor seemed to stretch in front of me like an image in a horror film.

I pushed myself up from my hands and knees and ran, stopping only when I thumped into the seat outside the Doctor's office.

I caught the chair before it toppled to the carpet. Tension made my head throb and distorted the door in front of me. I leaned against it for support. It gave way beneath my weight and I fell into the room with a gasp.

The Doctor's office was dark. A glimmer of moonlight shone through the window, but it wasn't going to be enough to see by. I shut my eyes, hoping they would adjust, but when I reopened them the desk remained nothing but a darker patch in the centre of the space. I glanced at the doorway.

'Seth?' I whispered. There was no answer.

I leaned against the wall and took a deep breath as I waited for my heart to slow. I was inside the office. No one knew I was there. I was safe . . . for now.

There was a blind on the window. If I closed it, then I could safely switch on the light.

I groped my way to the window and shut it as quietly as possible. Now I had to make my way back to the light switch in the pitch black. Abruptly my imagination filled the gloom with horrors and I broke into a sprint. My hip smacked into the edge of the desk and I bit off a scream as I bounced, disorientated, and staggered into a wall. Pressing one hand over the already swelling bruise and the other against the plaster I limped forward until I found the door frame.

I fumbled upwards, seeking the switch, all the time expecting something out of the shadows to grab my wrist, and the door opened next to me.

Instantly I stopped and held my breath. A figure slipped into the room. It was too dark to see who it was.

'Cass?'

It was Seth. Relief shook my breath free as he closed the door behind him. 'I'm here.' Quickly I clicked the light on, desperate to expel the silent dark.

'The door!' Seth too was in his pyjamas. He whipped off his top and stuffed it along the crack that would show the light to anyone looking down the corridor. The curve of his back was illuminated and, spontaneously, I threw my arms around him.

'We made it.'

'You're a genius, Cass.'

He turned, his arms tightened round me and I was suddenly very aware of his naked skin against my cotton sleepwear and the fact that I was wearing no bra.

'What's that?' Seth had spotted the chisel in the back of my trousers. Gratefully I freed it, using the action to release him and cover my embarrassment.

He nodded approvingly. 'Good idea.'

I handed it to him then went to sit in the Doctor's chair. Seth looked over my shoulder. There were three deep drawers in the desk and they were all locked.

I glanced at the chisel, but he shook his head. 'Let's look for a key before we do any damage.'

'Okay.' There were no obvious hiding places anywhere in the office. Feeling dejected I fiddled with the small, shallow drawer at the top of the desk. It opened.

My grin faded when I saw that it contained only a single spiral-bound notebook, biros, pencils, a sharpener and a highlighter. With only a little hope I opened the notebook. Only blanks remained.

Seth leaned over my shoulder. 'I had the last appointment today. She could have made some notes on the last page.' He plucked one of the pencils from the drawer and started to rub the lead on the next piece of paper. He was curved over me like a shell, his chest pressing against my back with gentle pressure. His bicep rubbed my arm as he coloured. I forced myself to focus on the paper.

When words actually started to appear shock almost knocked me off the seat. They were mostly garbled, some had pressed through from even earlier pages, but a few things had been written with enough force to be seen clearly.

David Curtiss Stephenson, Texas. <u>Near success.</u>
Close to emergence.
This lifetime.
Remains best prospect for fulfilment.
<u>Subject 8220 as back-up.</u>
Natural partnership with Grand Dragon.

I stared. 'Does that make any sense to you?'

Seth shook his head. 'There's no one called David here. Subject 8220 must be a patient ID, but I don't know whose.'

'What's a Grand Dragon?'

He shook his head more vigorously. 'I feel as if I should know, but I don't.'

'These notes can't be yours then.'

'I don't think so.'

My excitement vanished and I dumped my elbows on the desk. As I moved I knocked the laptop and it flickered to life. 'She left her computer on. No way!'

Eyes clamped to Seth's, I touched the keyboard and the screen brightened.

This computer is in use and has been locked. It may only be unlocked by the primary user or administrator. Press Ctrl-Alt-Del to enter password.

Seth's shoulders sagged but I looked at the paper in front of me.

I typed every single word we'd uncovered, but nothing happened. Resignedly I tried LEAZA then ASHWORTH and LEAZAASHWORTH just in case, but I remained locked out.

'Try MOUNT HERMON,' Seth suggested. It didn't work.

Frustration sizzled down my body and my right foot started to jiggle wildly. I moved my hand to one of the locked drawers but, before I could ask Seth for the chisel a floorboard shifted under my toes. Curious, I slid my feet around on the carpet but none of the other boards seemed loose. I slithered on to my knees under the desk.

'What're you doing?' Seth bent down, but I waved him back.

'I'm not sure.' I examined the carpet with my fingertips and found myself tracing a square in the pile. A memory came back to me: when I'd come into the Doctor's office earlier that day she had risen from beneath her desk.

I tucked my fingernails into the barely perceptible gap and peeled the tile back. It came away easily. Underneath, sure enough, there was a loose floorboard. I tried to lift it out.

'Ouch! I bent my nail back.'

Seth placed a firm hand on my shoulder. 'Let me try.'

I stood up so that he could take my place and he swiftly prised up the floor. As soon as he had the board out, I peered past him. Our efforts had revealed a small compartment and a wooden chest etched with the Doctor's logo: Orion's Belt.

Seth lifted the box out, holding it gingerly, like a bomb that had started to tick. I fell to my knees next to him. There was a terrible inevitability to its size.

Seth turned the box in his hands and the lid cracked open. It hadn't been locked. Breaths blending, we bent over it together.

The book was there, nested like a living thing in a mulch of felt and velvet. Just as I'd dreamed, the cover was black with age and the scaled binding was tough and brittle at the edges. It did not completely overlap all of the rough pages, which protruded like a mass of yellow tongues. I brushed my palm over the cover and recoiled. The leather felt slippery and organic.

'What kind of book hasn't got a title?' I whispered, wiping my hands on my trousers.

Nervously Seth licked his lips. 'A diary?'

Steeling myself I lifted the tome from the box and laid it on the floor between us. 'Let's find out.'

CHAPTER SEVENTEEN
THE BOOK

When Seth opened the blackened cover I saw that dozens of documents had been bound into the leather spine, like the snakes of Medusa's hair.

The first was so old that my fingertips trembled at the idea of touching it. It wasn't even paper. It reminded me of something I'd seen in a museum. I squinted at the odd symbols that covered the page, no more able to read it than I had been in my dream.

Seth's fingers hovered over the ink. 'This looks a bit like hieroglyphics,' he murmured. 'Kyle might recognise it.'

'You think Kyle would be able to read this?'

'It depends how close to the surface his Egyptian personality is. I can sometimes understand Yiddish.'

'And that's why I can speak German.'

'Yeah.' He made no further comment so I turned the pages, looking for familiar words.

The smell that drifted from the book reminded me of Pandra's hole: rotting flesh and desiccated corpses. I resisted the urge to cover my nose and skimmed over three more pages covered in pictograms. Then I came across yellowing parchment even more fragile.

We spent several minutes admiring the artistry of each capital letter. Although the crackling paper was starting to fall apart, the colours remained bright. Snakes and other serpents featured prominently, but stars also seemed to be important to the calligrapher.

'Orion's Belt, look.' Seth pointed.

'It's coming up everywhere,' I muttered.

Several pages later recognisable words began to stand out among the scrawl, but although we could decipher individuals, together they made no more sense than the odd words we'd pulled from the Doctor's notes.

I frowned over the faded ink of paper that became less fragile with each turn.

Seth caught my hand. 'Wait, I can read this. It's cramped but look . . . it's pretty close to modern English.'

Our heads almost touched as I traced the words with my finger and murmured them aloud.

* * *

Shemhazai and Azael, two angels in God's confidence, spoke to the Lord asking: 'Lord of the Universe, did we not warn You that man would prove unworthy of Your world? Are we not worthy to inherit Your world?'

God answered: 'Upon descending to Earth, you would sin even worse than man.'

They pleaded: 'Let us dwell there awhile, and we will make Your name sacred once more!'

God bound them with a law that prevented them from harming the sons of man. Then because He loved them dearly He allowed them to descend to Mount Hermon.

Seth's sharp inhalation curbed my recital. 'Mount Hermon,' he parroted.

I frowned. 'Why d'you think the Doctor named the Manor after the place angels came to earth?'

Seth shrugged. 'Because she liked the name . . .'

'It must be more than that.'

'Maybe her family comes from there or something.'

'Or something . . .' I found my place and read on.

* * *

233

> When he saw the beautiful daughters of man, Shemhazai was at once overcome by lust. He fathered two hundred monstrous sons.
>
> Each daily consumed a thousand camels, a thousand horses and a thousand oxen.

Seth's lips twitched. 'Two hundred sons! He was a busy guy.'

My stomach felt as if a hole had opened in it. 'He wasn't a guy. He was an angel.'

'It's only a story.' Seth squeezed my hand, but I pulled free. The words I had read seared into my brain.

'What's the matter?' Seth frowned.

'Don't you feel this might be . . . true?'

Seth rubbed his elbows. 'Maybe you shouldn't read any more.'

'No, I want to.' Ignoring his concern I muttered my way through the text to the next section.

> Azael's jealousy of man was so great that he invented the ornaments and cosmetics used by women to lead men astray. Then he taught man all manner of art to tempt women and created musical instruments to help with their seduction.

Then he said: 'Lord, see how lustful man is. See how ignorant he is of Your word. Destroy him and we can inherit Your world.'

But the Lord still loved the sons of Adam and He replied: 'No.'

So Azael brewed beer, gathered crowds in taverns and taught them to forge iron swords and spear-points with which to murder each other when they were drunk.

He said: 'Lord release us from Your law so that we might punish these men.'

But God knew that Azael had led man astray and would not release him.

And Azael was filled with bitterness and anger.

'There's something about that name, Azael.' Seth frowned.

He was right; my neck prickled as if something was trying to draw my attention. I traced the lettering with my fingertip and the ink smeared. I snatched my hand away, wiped my hand on my pyjama bottoms and tried to read the cramped writing without it.

* * *

Weary of man's rejection of Him, God warned the angels that He would set loose a flood to destroy all men and beasts.

Azael rejoiced because he believed he and his brother must now inherit the Earth.

But God said to them: 'You polluted yourselves with the daughters of men and sinned within My sight. Your works and the tribes created by your lust will be destroyed and as long as Noah's heirs still praise My name, you will not inherit the Earth.'

Shemhazai wept bitterly. 'Surely, Lord, You do not mean to destroy my sons?'

And God replied: 'Your sons, sinners created by both flesh and spirit, will die. But their evil spirits will not die. After death their spirits will cause destruction on the Earth. They will rise up against the children of man, because it is they who brought the flood upon them, and they will never have rest.'

Filled with repentance for what his lust had unleashed Shemhazai asked the Lord if there was any hope for mankind.

The Lord replied: 'I will bind your sons into fleshly bodies for three hundred generations.'

* * *

Seth wrapped my fist in his. 'Some father. He just gave up on them.' He touched his scar and I stared at the page, discomfited.

'What did it mean the spirits would be bound into fleshly bodies? Were the ghosts of his sons made into humans?'

Seth's face twisted and for a second the mismatching of his eyes was even more acute. 'Christ, imagine the torture: being stuck inside a human body when they hated us so much.'

'But it meant they didn't die . . . No, I'm wrong, aren't I? Instead of drowning just once they each had to die three hundred times.'

Seth's eyes were haunted. 'Like our nightmares, but living it instead of dreaming it.'

'For how long? Let's say an average of twenty years per life then that's . . .' I paused, calculating. '*Six thousand years.*'

Strange and instant fury consumed me. I had to smash something. As if possessed I lurched towards the laptop on the desk. When my arm was wrenched behind me I jerked to a stop, surprised to find Seth holding on.

'I don't know what's happening.' His own face was mottled red and white. 'But we have to control these feelings.'

I dropped back to the floor, trying to ride out the emotion that would certainly give us away to the patrolling nurses, but it was like trying to surf in a hurricane.

'Why do I feel like this?' Frenzied tears boiled down my face. 'Why am I so *angry*?'

Seth wrapped his arms round me and squeezed as if he could pour his own wrath into my body.

'Seth,' I gasped into his collar bone. 'You're hurting me.'

I struggled to lift my head and found myself breathing into his mouth. Abruptly he rammed his lips on to mine with all the force of our combined fury.

Devoured: that was how I felt.

Then it was as if all the alien and violating rage changed focus. I dug my nails into Seth's back and raked his skin, gleeful as welts rose under my fingertips. The kiss deepened and I wanted to climb inside him, become one body. His hands touched my ribs, lifted my pyjama top and skimmed roughly over my burning skin. He sank his fists into my hair, tugging it roughly.

Then, just as suddenly as the kiss had begun, his touch gentled; our rage had been driven out by fever-bright desire.

Slowly our kisses lightened and we drew apart.

I touched my swollen lips and stared at his. My chin was raw, scraped by the shadow of stubble on his cheeks. We were both shaking.

'Cass, I'm so sorry.' Seth winced and I realised that I'd really hurt his back. 'I don't think we should read any more.' He slid away from me. 'It's like something is waking up inside me . . . and it's furious.' He swallowed.

'Are you kidding?' I pushed back my hair. 'Could you really leave now? Don't you want to know what just happened to us?'

'What if it gets worse?' Seth's hands shook like an old man's. 'I might not be able to control myself next time.'

'I have to know.' I attempted to steady my gaze and my limbs, trying to communicate to him that I had enough control for the both of us.

Finally Seth nodded, so I read on.

Shemhazai knelt before the Lord and thanked him for his mercy.

And the Lord set Shemhazai in the southern sky, a star between Heaven and Earth, head down, feet up.

Then He spoke: 'Heaven shall remain closed to you and your brother. Unless the spirits you created in your lust overcome the restrictions of their fleshly bodies you will remain in this prison until the end of the world.'

Then the Lord sought Azael. But Azael was fearful. Believing that the Lord would be unable to see an angel in human form he took the shape he hated most. Then he vowed to find the sons of his brother and aid them in the destruction of man.

The text ended and I came back to myself to find my fists beneath my chin. Although the unfathomable rage threatened to return it had already exhausted my adrenaline and I was able to drive the weakened emotion down.

Seth leaned forward, trembling. 'What if they overcome the restrictions of their human bodies? What happens then?'

I turned the page, but that was the end of the legend.

Why do I care? A hundred or so years ago a crackpot religious guy wrote a story, that's all.

But that wasn't all . . . and I knew it. I looked at Seth.

'Don't say it.' He glowered. 'Don't even think it.'

'It makes sense.'

'No it doesn't. *We aren't the sons of Shemhazai.*'

'Seth . . .'

'It's just a story. Maybe the Doctor has it because it's an early attempt to explain reincarnation.'

'We've lived who knows how many past lives. The book says his sons won't rest and *we never rest.*'

He jumped up as if he'd forgotten his own reaction to the text. 'I think we should leave.'

I bit my lip. 'I'm going to go through the rest of the book . . . see if there's any better explanation.'

Seth huffed and began to prowl restlessly around the office. I ignored his activity; all I could think about was the story. Seth was wrong. It wasn't a legend – it was history.

Chapter Eighteen
REVELATION

As I read on, the book appeared to turn into a diary after all. The later pages, no longer a set of mismatched manuscripts, were covered with odd comments and smudged notes.

Many were instructions on how to worship the angel Shemhazai, and I flicked through with only mild interest. Then something struck me.

'Seth, this is written from Azael's point of view. It's his book. Listen: *My repellent disguise shields me from His sight. As long as I do not call His name He cannot find me.* The legend said Azael hid from God, remember?'

Seth stopped his restless pacing. 'A lot of writers tell stories from another viewpoint. It's called fiction.'

'What about this? I have discovered that my brother is set in the heavens, in the constellation that the Greeks call Orion.'

Seth hesitated. 'Orion?'

'That's where Shemhazai is supposed to be. Seth . . . I see the image of Orion everywhere.'

He licked his lips nervously. 'It's a coincidence.'

Like a fly to one of Pandra's corpses my eyes were drawn to a sentence underlined in black: _The search for the trapped spirits must be a priority._ _My priests and I will find Shemhazai's sons. Together we will destroy man and turn his faith in the Lord to dust. Then my brother will be freed and together we will inherit the Earth._

I flicked back and forth through the notes.

An ache in my jaw warned me that I was grinding my teeth. 'According to this, Azael plans to destroy man . . . or at least his belief in God. He would have to do something really big to do that, wouldn't he? Like . . . natural-disaster big. Huge enough to make people say no God would let it happen.'

Seth chewed his swollen knuckle and his eyes met mine. 'My last incarnation was during the Second World War.'

'Mine too.' I swallowed. 'Do you . . . do you think that could have been caused by Azael?'

'If it was, he failed. A lot of people still have faith.'

'So . . . before the six thousand years are up, he'll have to use the sons to do something even worse.' I swallowed. 'How old do you think those early manuscripts are?'

Seth fingered the chisel. 'This is crazy.'

'Listen. *Before my brother can be released, his sons must be guided to lustful and murderous acts. They must not be thwarted by conscience nor the human laws that bind them.*'

Seth snorted.

'What?'

He shook his head. 'The legend says Shemhazai will be released once his children overcome *the restrictions of their fleshly bodies.* Lust and murder isn't rising above humanity – it's more like giving in to it.'

'So . . . what would they need to do?'

'Um . . . act more like angels than men. So maybe praying . . . repenting for their sins, like Shemhazai did. I'd guess Shemhazai will be trapped in Orion's Belt until his sons are sorry for all the bad stuff they've done.'

'Then Azael has it wrong.'

Seth shrugged. 'He probably wanted revenge so badly he couldn't make out the real meaning of the words. If his sons had asked for forgiveness, Shemhazai would have been released.'

'But if Azael's turning them into killers . . .'

'. . . Shemhazai will be trapped forever and the spirits of his sons will never be free.'

He's stopped talking as if this is just a story.

With a jolt I remembered that the Doctor had been writing in the book. With fingers that felt like someone else's I flipped to the end. I honestly hoped to find some sort of scholarly comment on the text, some reason that she might have the book other than the one I feared.

The back pages were blank, waiting to be written to life, so I started to search backwards. About twenty pages from the end, I found the most recent of her notes.

I didn't understand them. Each entry was headed by a number and had two or three lines of writing underneath. Other numbers followed and then a thick line marked the next entry. I read the most recent.

8220: F. b. 1992. EN. Shows early promise. Ref. 7999.

'Seth, look. Wasn't that number 8220 on the notepad?'

Seth slid the pencil blackened paper from the desk. 'Yes. It says *"Subject 8220 as back-up".*'

'I was last in to the Manor and 8220 is the last entry. So I could be subject 8220.' I narrowed my eyes. 'Who am I supposed to back up?'

Once more behind me Seth shook his head. 'Ref. 7999. What does it say under that number?'

I flicked backwards until I found 7999 at the head of an entry:

7999: M. b. 1920. DE. Shows early promise. Ref. 5329.

Moved into stage two. Ref. 5200.

d. 1944 before emergence.

I heard him swallow. 'I think "d" stands for died. He died in 1944.'

'Does that mean "b" is born? Born 1920, died 1944. What's stage two?'

He shook his head. 'I don't know. Look at the one above. He got to stage three.'

'Why he?'

'The "M".' He reached over me, returned the book to my own entry and pointed to *8220: F.* 'The "F" here must stand for "female".'

'I was born in 1992.'

'Let's see the earliest entries.' Seth paged back until we reached the start of the notes and I felt the tension race through him. 'Look at the dates, Cass.'

'It says "BC". That can't be right.' My fingers trembled over the ink.

'These notes have been copied in from an earlier document.' Seth's voice was brittle as old bones.

I turned to frown at him. 'How do you know?'

He shrugged. 'People wouldn't have said "BC" then, would they? They'd have used a different dating system. And look – the writing's the same on these pages: the same pen; the same hand. Someone copied them in later.' He sucked air through his teeth as he flicked forward. Finally he stopped. 'Here's where they started entering notes as events occurred. It's a different pen for each entry and they've all faded differently.'

'So . . . 1916 . . . that's when this book was made.'

'Seems like it.'

My head pounded with the effort of making sense of the scrawl, but something else was screaming for my attention. I tried to relax, to open myself up to the insistent thought. I stared at the open book until my eyes lost focus.

'Seth, where's that piece of paper?'

Wordlessly he handed it down to me. I stared at the page covered with the Doctor's handwriting. Then my eyes flicked between the page in my hand and the notes in the book.

'Do you see it?'

'Move over.' Seth dropped to his knees beside me.

'The writing's the same.'

'It can't be.' He nodded at the paper in my hand. 'That's the Doctor's handwriting.'

'I-I know.' I met his stunned gaze and flipped back to the ancient legend itself.

It too had been written in the Doctor's hand.

'It's not possible.' Seth swiped his hand over his face. 'We're seeing things because we're tired.'

'Look at the "f" and "t". They don't change.'

'We're not experts.' But his voice cracked.

Then something else struck me with numbing force. 'Look at the Doctor's name. Leaza Ashworth. Azael . . . Leaza.' The paper slipped out of my fingers and fluttered to the floor. 'The *Doctor* is *Azael.*'

'Don't be ridiculous.' Seth jumped to his feet. He backed away as if I'd grown horns. 'Listen to yourself. You seriously think we're the reincarnation of the sons of one fallen angel and that our Doctor is another one who wants to use us to destroy the human race?' His hands covered his face and he stopped talking. When he dropped them he was calmer. 'Anyway, the Doctor's a woman.'

I sighed. 'You're right, I'm sure you are. It's just, the handwriting, her name, the story, our dreams . . . they all add up.' I paused. 'Maybe it's why I hate Lenny so much. I didn't know why. I've been beating myself up over it, but if Shemhazai's sons hate the weakness of humanity . . . well, Lenny is so weak . . .'

Seth buckled into the Doctor's chair and I saw how exhausted he was, how tired we both were. Maybe I wasn't thinking straight.

Then I gasped. 'Oh my God . . . Seth, we have to get out of here.'

He nodded. 'Yes. Put the book back. We need to think this through.'

'No. I mean we've got to get out of the Manor and we have to get the others out too.'

Seth blinked. 'You're crazy.'

'Maybe. That doesn't matter now. More importantly: is the Doctor crazy?' Seth's eyes widened but I carried on, hammering home my point. 'It doesn't matter if the Doctor *is* Azael, or if she just believes she is. If she wrote this . . . and I'm sure she did . . . then she thinks we're Shemhazai's children. So what do you think she's doing to us with all her *therapy*?'

Seth's arms flopped bonelessly to his sides. 'The Doctor's trying to take away our consciences. The crazy bitch isn't trying to help us at all; she's trying to turn us into killers.'

'Look what damage she's done to Pandra already.' Shuddering, I pictured her secret place.

'Alright, I agree. We have to get out of here.'

I thought about all the treatments I'd had in this very room and felt ill. 'How can we get the others out without the nurses stopping us?'

Seth drummed his nails on the leather blotter. Then his eyes glittered. 'Lizzie's game . . . Double Dares. We'll dare the others to break out with us and come to the village pub. We can tell them about the book once we get there.'

I nodded; it sounded good. 'But . . . that won't work for Pandra.'

His shoulders sagged. 'She won't do anything I suggest.' He paused. 'We could just leave her.'

'We can't. She's probably in the most danger and you know it.' My hands were cold. I rubbed them together. 'Also, I'm fairly sure the blockers won't work on the outside door. We need her key card.'

Seth frowned. 'Why not just use one of ours?'

I hesitated, still reluctant to expose Pandra's secret. 'You're the one who said Pandra's like the Doctor's daughter. She's allowed in and out of the Manor pretty much as she wants. If we use Pandra's card, I don't think an alarm will be raised. If we use yours or mine . . .'

'. . . They'll be after us in a shot.' Seth's expression was grim.

'I can get her to take me outside. She'll open the exterior door in the rec room and I'll block it with something before it shuts. You can all sneak out behind us.'

Seth's palm rasped over his cheeks. 'We'd be tramping around the moor without a map.'

I shivered at the thought. 'We can follow the road to the village.'

'But if the Doctor finds us gone it's the first place she'll look.' Seth rested his forearms on the desk and groaned. 'Even if we get away our parents will probably send us straight back.' He looked at the book. 'We'll have to take it with us. No one would send us back here once they saw those notes.'

Alarm rippled through me. 'She might look for it tomorrow. If she finds out it's gone . . .'

Seth closed his eyes. 'We have to take it. If we come back for it, we might get caught.'

I wiped my hands on the brushed cotton of my pyjamas. Then before I could change my mind, I stuffed the empty box back into its hiding place and scooped up the book. My flesh crawled. The hole under the desk and Pandra's secret place seemed nothing alike on the surface but to me they felt identical; both contained horrors.

Seth followed me to the door and switched off the light. The office plunged into darkness and his trousers rustled as he bent to retrieve his top from the floor.

'Don't forget the blocker,' I whispered. As Seth palmed it I ducked into the corridor. The rectangle of light on the carpet had brightened. Dawn was approaching.

Pyjamas flapping, Seth and I ran towards the staircase. Then he held me behind him as he peered through the glass panel. 'The stairs are empty.' He pushed the door open and lifted the second wooden block.

I followed him through at a dash and we sped up the staircase. I barely thought about stealth. Now we were this far I just wanted to be back in the relative safety of my room and the book out of my arms.

At the top of the stairs Seth stopped. Swiftly he pulled me close and pressed his lips to mine. Between us the book pressed uncomfortably into my breasts.

'Get some sleep,' he whispered huskily. Then he pushed me towards the girls' area.

The sight of my door filled me with near joy. Briefly I looked for Seth but he had already disappeared so I took a deep breath and half fell into my room.

I had to find somewhere to stash the book. Finally I decided to hide it inside my rucksack. There it seemed to whisper its story with a sort of malevolent seductiveness so I tucked the bag into the back of my wardrobe and threw myself into bed.

Wretchedly I wrapped my arms around Bunny and tucked my face against his fur. But as I dug my fingers into my old toy my eyes fell on the buttons by the bed.

The recorder! I can't leave it empty.

Anxiously I pressed the button. I'd talk about Zillah. My breathlessness should be put down to the usual nightmare. It would be as if I'd never left my bed.

* * *

When I finally slumped back on to the mattress I glanced at the clock. The figures danced and blurred.

If I sleep now, I'll be able to snatch a couple of hours before breakfast.

I closed my eyes but like a computer hard drive my brain wouldn't stop whirring. All I could see was an extract from the book: *They will rise up against the children of man . . . and they will never have rest.*

PART FOUR

INSURRECTION

'Believing that the Lord would be unable to see an angel in human form he took the shape he hated most. Then he vowed to find the sons of his brother and aid them in the destruction of man.'

CHAPTER NINETEEN

ESCAPE

I could barely keep my eyes open. I needed to sleep before the day's appointments, or who knew what I'd say? As soon as I'd choked down my breakfast and the nurse had seen me take my drugs I started back to my room.

As I was passing the phone booth Seth grabbed my arm, pulled me inside and pressed his mouth to my ear. 'I've spoken to the others and they're up for the dare.'

I gave myself a mental shake. 'Will everyone have blockers?'

'Lizzie's making them right now.'

I rubbed my sore eyes. 'So, we're doing this today.'

Seth nodded and his arms tightened round me. 'Tonight. We'll meet behind the tennis courts at ten, after the nurse's rounds.' He released me and I stumbled. 'Did you sleep?'

I looked at Seth. It was obvious that he hadn't. His skin looked like the ash at the bottom of a burnt-out fire.

Do I look that bad?

I bit off my concern.

I had a job to do. I had to persuade Pandra to take me back to her secret place.

I found her reading in her room.

'Pandra, can I go out with you tonight?'

'What?' Pandra shut her book and stared. I tilted my head, curious to see what it was. I made out the words 'Darren Shan' and shivered; some of the boys at school read his stuff.

'I-I have to do something.' I bit my lip. 'I had terrible nightmares last night. The worst. I want to go back there.'

Pandra toyed with the bar through her eyebrow. 'You want to go into the woods?'

I made sure the corridor was empty. 'To your secret place, yes.'

'Tonight?'

I allowed a note of pleading into my voice. 'You said it helped.'

'It does.'

I stepped further into her room and the wallpaper of screaming faces surrounded me. She measured my sincerity with a long look then grinned. 'Alright, you're on.'

'Shall I knock for you at quarter to ten?'

'Cool.' She grinned enthusiastically. 'You're gonna love this. We'll have so much fun.'

The rest of the day I avoided speaking to Seth. I was terrified that if I so much as looked in his direction I'd give us away. Every time a nurse entered the room I jumped, certain the Doctor had discovered our theft of the book. Yet as the day went on and no alarm was raised I got more and more wound up.

It was hard to ignore the energy that seethed around the others. Max was excited about seeing 'a British pub', Kyle just wanted to leave the Manor for a bit and Lizzie was delighted with the fact that Seth was finally joining her game.

When she bounced up to me at tea-time and pressed a palm-sized wooden wedge into my hand I nodded but said nothing. By that point my teeth ached with the tension, as if my jaw had been wired together, and I wasn't sure I could open my mouth even if I wanted to.

I headed to my room as soon after that as I could and set my alarm for nine thirty p.m. I'd only managed to nap for about half an hour earlier and although I couldn't face the idea of another nightmare I knew my body, at least, desperately needed some rest.

The pieces of the gun gleam in the dawn light that shines through the high window. My cleaning cloth, now smeared and oily, is on the floor next to the table. I crack my knuckles and wait for the signal. Oberleutnant Fleischer slaps his baton on the table and I snatch my extractor up an instant before the others puts their hands on theirs.

I slide the channel over the lug and click the safety into the rear of the bolt sleeve. My fingers perform the familiar movements without thought and as I slide the main spring on to the rear of the firing pin Hans remains a beat behind me.

I stab the wooden block with the tip of the pin and compress the spring. As I return the cocking sleeve to the rear of the firing pin there's a curse and a crash. Heinrich has fumbled and his spring has released too early. Grinning, I carefully allow the main spring and bolt sleeve to expa...'

As I insert the firing pin assembly into the back end of the bolt body I inhale the scent of grease on metal that is so beautiful to me. Abruptly another scent winds round that of the oil.

I turn like a puppet. Frau Asche is watching us assemble our weapons from the back of the room. The slick of crimson on her smiling lips is the only spot of colour on her otherwise perfectly pale face.

What is she doing here? Oberleutnant Fleischer had made it clear that our preparations for this mission were to be kept secret.

My fingers are oily and suddenly I feel clumsy but, thankfully. I have no small pieces left to deal with. Directing concentration back to my task I deftly rotate the sleeve and extractor, insert the bolt into the rifle's receiver and shut it.

Click. I move the safety from the middle position and slam the weapon down to indicate that I am done.

The crash of Hans's gun is an echo of mine. My eyes go to the clock above the Oberleutnant's shoulder. Less than fifty seconds have passed. I hide a smirk beneath my sleeve. No one is faster than me at assembling a gun.

Oberleutnant Fleischer nods his approval and gestures us to the trucks outside.

At nine forty-five I stood outside Pandra's door wearing my Converse with two pairs of socks, my warmest clothes and my winter coat. My rucksack was slung over my shoulder but I was taking only the book and things I couldn't replace, like Bunny.

I took a deep breath and knocked quietly. The door swung open.

'You planning on moving in?' Eyes on my bag Pandra grinned and I couldn't help smiling back.

'Just a few things I thought we might need.' I shrugged the rucksack higher on my back and willed her to accept my explanation.

Pandra shrugged and led the way to the end of the corridor. We marched past the football table in the rec room and paused at the outside door long enough for Pandra to palm her key card. I kept my eyes fixed on her back, worried that if I looked around I might give the others away.

While Pandra worked the lock I took Lizzie's wedge from my coat pocket.

'Let's go.' Pandra pushed open the door and I held my hand behind my back.

As she stepped into the near dark I crouched, as if to check my laces, and jammed the slice of wood into the door frame. With any luck it would hold until Seth removed it on his way past.

Pandra and I walked towards the wood, keeping the new shooting range on our right. Although I tried not to picture the equipment that would be secured in there, the ghost of a gun stock pressed against my palm. Abruptly dizzy, I closed my fist round it.

The feel of the phantom gun brought Zillah back to me and now I seemed to hear her voice echoing between the trees ahead.

I ignored her. I had to distract Pandra, or she might notice the others following us.

'So . . . how much longer do you reckon you'll be at the Manor?'

Pandra blinked. 'Until I'm cured I guess.'

'Then what will you do?'

She focused on the wet grass. 'I was hoping the Doctor might keep me on as an assistant or something. There'll be some work I could do . . .'

'What about school?'

'I won't need school.'

We had reached the edge of the wood and I no longer imagined I could hear Zillah's ghostly cries. I cleared my throat. 'Maybe you could come and stay with me for a while.'

Pandra stared. 'You'd be alright with that? After yesterday I figured you wouldn't want to be friends any more.'

'I was just . . . shocked, that's all.' I caught her arm as she started into the trees.

'Why've we stopped?' She frowned.

'We need to talk about something else.'

She tried to pull away. 'Can't we talk in the cave?'

'No.' I bit the inside of my cheek; I'd been worrying about this conversation all day. 'Do you trust me?'

Thoughtfully Pandra nodded. 'You didn't tell any of the others about my place and after you left like that I thought you would.' I let my grip on her arm relax and Pandra's eyes sparkled. 'I knew you'd come round; it's like we're sisters or something.'

Given Pandra's background, I was willing to bet that meant even more to her than it did to me. My traitorous heart pumped, convinced I was about to betray her.

If the legend in the book is true, then we sort of are family.

My mind skittered away from the thought and Pandra nodded towards the woods. 'Ready to go?'

I held on to her coat. 'Not yet.' I didn't dare glance past her to see if the others were on their way. 'I-I found something in the Doctor's office.'

Pandra frowned but made no move to leave. 'There isn't anything in the Doctor's office.'

'I found a book . . . under her floorboards.'

She fiddled with her eyebrow piercing. 'How'd you find *anything* under her floorboards?'

'That isn't important; the book is. It scared me.'

'What is it, a horror story?'

I shuffled my feet. 'It's more like a religious legend crossed with an instruction manual . . . finished with a load of strange notes.'

Pandra fidgeted. 'So?'

'I think you need to see it – I think we all do.'

With obvious scepticism she said one long drawn-out, 'Okay.'

'The thing is . . . we can't do it here . . . and we can't take the others to your secret place.' Finally I looked past her and saw the small band trooping after us across the field. Now that I knew they were coming I could hear Belinda's excited whispers.

'No bloody way!'

Prepared for Pandra to bolt I was already tightening my grip. 'I know I said I wanted to go to your secret place, but you wouldn't have come out otherwise. I have to show you this.'

'You never really wanted me to move in with you, did you?' She yanked her arm free and loathing warped her face.

'It's not like that . . .'

'Show me this book now and I can go back in.'

The ice in Pandra's voice pierced my heart, but I couldn't let her return to the Manor and rat us out. I lowered my voice. 'I went with you to your place. I could tell the others about it right now.' I let that thought fester between us until her frown deepened, then I continued: 'They'd be horrified. I bet Seth would call the police. What would they think about it?' Pandra's face blanched. Swiftly I carried on speaking. 'All I want is for you to come and read the book. After that you can do whatever you like.' I tried to smile at her, but my lips would barely curl. 'It might even be fun to go to the pub.'

'With them?' she spat.

'We all have to see the book.'

At that point Seth reached us. 'Hello, Pandra, nice of you to join us.'

Our feet crunched on the gravel driveway and the low sound of excited chatter soaked into the deepening gloom. Silently I let my arm slip into Pandra's; partly for balance, but also because I was worried she might try to sneak back to the Manor once it was completely dark.

When we reached the sign for Mount Hermon Seth switched

on his torch. Shadows crowded creepily around the small island of light and I shuddered and looked for the moon.

Scrawls of cloud decorated the sky, crayoned over random constellations. Was it going to rain? Immediately thoughts of flash floods crowded my mind.

'Which way?' Seth swung the beam left and right. 'Do you remember?'

I swallowed. *I can't turn back now. All we have to do is follow the road to the village and this'll all be over.*

'Left,' I said. 'Harmon village is left.'

We set off.

Having become used to the scrunch of gravel, the near silence of the road made me twitchy. Sensitive as broken teeth, my ears were waiting for the sound of rushing water, so a sudden rustling in the verge caused me to tighten my grip on Pandra's arm.

'Stop being pathetic,' she sneered.

My cheeks burned but, before I could answer, Lizzie shrieked and Seth swung his torch towards her feet.

The beam picked out the remains of some enormous road kill and I jumped.

Oh my God, it's a badger.

Lizzie stared wide-eyed at the dead animal and Kyle made retching sounds as he wiped his feet on a patch of grass.

He must have trodden in it.

'Oh, gross.' Belinda's voice came from just behind me, but she drifted closer to the animal, tucking her hair behind her ears, her face a study in fascination.

'That's disgusting.' Lenny danced on his toes behind Seth, as if the road could contaminate him.

I was suddenly very much aware of the book in my bag and, despite the cold, my palms started to sweat.

'Are you alright, Cass?' Seth's voice shattered my focus and I glanced at Pandra with a shiver. She was smiling.

Out here the stars shone so much brighter than they did at home and it seemed that the further we walked from Mount Hermon, the more dazzling they became. Finally I stopped, forcing Pandra to a halt, and stared upwards.

Seth joined us. 'What is it?'

I gestured. 'Look at the sky – it's incredible.'

Through the shifting knots of cloud Orion's Belt shone like diamonds on velvet and I could clearly make out the Plough, pointing to Polaris and bright Cassiopeia.

'Can we keep moving? I'm cold.'

Belinda's complaint harmonised with Lenny's. 'Me too. I'm *freezing*.'

Despite my instinct to argue with anything Lenny said, I had to agree. The chill was insidious and my clothing felt like tissue paper under the blowtorch of frigid wind. Even Seth's teeth were chattering.

We started forward again but my feet tingled inside my trainers and I knew they'd soon be numb. Pandra said nothing but her arm in mine was rigid with cold.

'I'm beat.' Max stumbled to a stop. 'Maybe we should do this another time.'

I glanced at Seth and shifted my rucksack to a more comfortable position, trying not to think about the book that lay in the bottom like a ticking bomb.

'You'll forfeit the dare, Max.' Lizzie grinned. 'You know the rules.'

Seth waved his arm towards the endless black road. 'C'mon, Max. It can't be much further. I'll buy you a Red Bull when we get there.'

Max's lips narrowed. 'Fine, but we're getting a cab back.'

'This isn't New York.' Lizzie laughed. 'I don't think there're any taxis around here.'

He glared. 'Well, maybe someone'll give us a ride.'

The wind fell away and I tuned out their bickering. Once more I looked up and this time water splattered on my cheek. As I watched, the moon vanished behind the clouds. What had, only a short while ago, been an infant scrawl of grey had turned into a star-smothering blanket.

An icy gust blew up my jacket and swirled my hair across my face. The wind had returned.

I dug my nails into Pandra's arm and felt her stiffen. 'Th-there's a storm coming,' I gasped.

'I know.' She pulled my hand off her arm. 'It was on the forecast. I thought we'd be in the cave by now.'

Frantically I looked around, as if shelter would magically appear, but there was nothing to see in the rustling darkness. My voice rose to a shriek. 'We have to get inside.'

Realising something was wrong Seth turned the light on me. Already the beam was spotted with thick drizzle and I wrapped my arms round myself, thoughts crackling with fear.

'Cass?'

'She doesn't want to get wet,' Pandra sneered.

'That's not it.' Seth drew closer. 'Are you alright?'

'There's a storm coming.' I could barely force out the words. I swayed and bursts of German whirled through my head like static. 'The Doctor said . . . flash floods . . . We could d-drown.'

'Fear of drowning . . . that's her trigger? I didn't realise.' Distantly I saw Pandra's eyes meet Seth's; it was the first time I'd heard her speak to him without naked hostility. 'I've seen this guy take over before. He's strong.'

'If he decides to run, she could get lost on the moor.' Seth grabbed my shoulders. 'Cass, hold on in there. We'll walk faster. The village can't be much further.'

I shuddered as I recalled all the little outposts we'd need to pass before we reached the village. We hadn't yet seen a single one. I shook my head frantically. 'We've got to get to high ground.'

Kyle used the light on his mobile phone to illuminate the impenetrable verges. 'There isn't anywhere to go, man. It won't be safe to leave the road.'

Seth nodded and gave me another shake. 'We'll be alright. We have to keep walking.'

Thunder rumbled in the distance and I choked on a scream.

Seth held me so close that I could feel his heart beating through our jackets. 'We have to keep going, Cass.' I shook my head again, near hysterical, and he whispered in my ear. 'Do you want to go back to the Manor?'

His words were like a bucket of ice down my back.

The Doctor will be waiting for us.

Another roll of thunder shook the world and Seth spoke into my hair. 'Come on, Cass. I won't let anything happen to you.'

I forced a nod and looked at my feet. 'I c-can't move.'

Seth yanked me alongside him and I fell into his side. My legs swung stiffly at first then speeded up.

Lizzie and Kyle went on ahead with his phone. Abruptly Kyle ran back to us shouting to be heard over the wind. 'There's something here.'

Seth raised his torch and relief almost knocked me over. We had reached Hope Farm.

ZILLAH

S eth shouted but there was no answer.

 'It's deserted.' He peered into the kitchen, his hands held against the window.

I huddled beneath the lintel and clutched at a rusty drainpipe. A waterfall gushed from the spout and soaked my toes. I watched the foam until my eyes lost their focus and the world started to whirl like a fairground ride.

'We aren't going to get to the pub, are we?' Belinda joined me and started to wring water out of her coat. 'I think we should go back.' I looked up in time to see her glare defiantly at Lizzie. 'And I don't think we should have to do one of your dumb forfeits.'

Seth turned to her. 'We need to wait out the storm. We'll talk about going back once it's died down.'

I ducked my chin into my coat. 'C-can we get in?'

Seth tried the door. 'It's locked up tight.'

Kyle stood next to him. His clothes were black as usual and his disembodied face floated ghoulishly in the shadows. 'We could break a window.'

Seth shook his head. 'I'm just going to walk around the property.' He looked at me. 'Stay right here.'

'Wait.' Lizzie ran to his side. 'Double Dares is my game. I'll come with you.'

I leaned against the cold stone, watched the rain come down and tried to stifle the voice that urged me to run.

Nonchalantly Pandra propped herself on the wall just outside the cover, simultaneously flaunting her indifference to the rain and guarding my escape route.

Lenny huddled at Kyle's side. The older boy glanced down crossly. 'Get under cover, man.'

Lenny shook his head and pointed at me. 'Not while she's in there.'

'It isn't much drier under here anyway, not with this wind,' Belinda moaned, and flicked her blonde hair.

Devoted Max swiftly undid his jacket and spread it out, sheltering her from the soaking gusts.

After a long silence, broken only by the rumbling and hissing of the storm, the door cracked open.

Lizzie peered out at us from the dark hole. 'We found an unlocked window,' she whispered.

'Come inside, quick.' Seth appeared behind her and held his hand out to me. I grabbed it like a lifeline and just as lightning turned the abandoned farm into a photo negative I ducked through the door.

Seth guided us through a narrow kitchen. I held my head as I walked behind him. The quivering torchlight made the walls seem to spin and I felt as if I was about to fall into the greasy range.

'Why don't we just switch on a light?' Belinda wanted to know.

Lizzie answered her. 'We're breaking and entering, dummy.'

Seth whispered over the sound of Belinda's indignant inhalation. 'We can put a light on at the back of the house. We just don't want anyone to see it from the road.'

Outside the kitchen we found ourselves corralled by doors warped with age and damp.

Seth aimed the torch and we ducked through the sagging corridor into a sitting room where the worn carpet barely absorbed the sound of our feet.

Immediately my eyes went to the window and Seth pulled the

curtains, hiding my view of the pounding rain. As he did so, Belinda found the light switch.

Under the electric glow I immediately felt less disorientated. The single unforgiving bulb showed a blue cord sofa that oozed stuffing and, in front of the grate, a red rug thick with patches of dog hair. It wasn't exactly homely, but it was safe.

Exhaustion anchored me in place and I watched, uncaring, as Belinda claimed the couch. She looked pointedly at Max and he laid his coat, wet side down, on the cushions. Max perched on the arm, as close to her as possible and with a creaking of springs Lizzie took the other spot on the sofa.

Bonelessly I folded on to the floor where I stood, too weary even to remove my wet coat. Seth knelt next to me and wrapped his arm round my shoulders. I looked up, surprised, then relaxed into the crook of his elbow.

'Well, this *is* nice,' Belinda said sarcastically

'Any chance of lighting the fire, do you think?' Kyle dropped on to the rug next to Lenny and looked wistfully at the soot-blackened grate.

Seth shook his head. 'Now we're here, Cass and I have something to show you.'

Curious faces turned to me as I fumbled my rucksack open and removed the book.

'What is it?' Belinda leaned forward. Then she screamed as if I'd shoved a box of tarantulas in her face.

'What the *hell*?' Max grabbed her, but his own cheeks were ice white. 'Where did you get that?'

Lizzie and Kyle wore matching expressions of horror. Lenny crawled forward to see better and his mouth fell open. 'I-it's *the book*,' he whispered.

I let Seth answer. 'We found it in the Doctor's office. It belongs to her.'

Only Pandra didn't react.

'Pandra?' I whispered.

She ignored me. 'Are you going to read it, or what?'

Seth opened the book at the retelling of the legend. He hesitated then offered it to Pandra.

She half dropped it on the floor in front of her, wiped her fingers on her jeans and began to read out loud.

The words of the book, once spoken, seemed to crowd into the air around the room, and made the space feel more cramped by the moment. The storm drew nearer as the paragraphs soaked into the air around me, turning the room from a cosy bolt-hole to a lamp-lit pit.

Eventually Pandra's voice started to hoarsen. When she reached the pages of notes she flicked through as confused as I had been, then slammed the book shut and kicked it across the floor. The ancient text bounced once and landed face up on the rug like a broken bird. Then she turned on me. 'You don't believe any of this, do you?'

Outside, the storm had settled into a heavy rain. It battered the windows like a besieging sea. 'I don't think it matters,' I muttered. 'What matters is – does the Doctor believe it?'

Lizzie's hands covered her mouth. 'You mean . . . the Doctor wants us to try and free some trapped angel?' Her brown eyes were wide over the smudges of exhaustion that marked us all like brands. 'Can she make us do . . . those terrible things?'

Seth nodded. 'We think so.'

Finally Lenny spoke. 'I'm not an evil spirit,' he whispered. His voice could barely be heard over the cackling of the rain.

Lizzie leaned towards him. 'Of course you aren't. None of us are!' She glared around, defying anyone to disagree.

Kyle rubbed his hair into wet black spikes. 'The point, man, is that the *Doctor* thinks some of us might be. She's using the treatment to turn us into . . . killing machines.'

'So, she's a fraud.' Max's shoulders slumped and his voice dropped so low I could barely hear him. 'Do you know what I gave up back home to come here?'

Kyle blinked. 'If she's a fake . . . does that mean we don't have past lives?'

Belinda rubbed her eyes, acting more like a normal little girl than I'd ever seen her. 'If we aren't reincarnating . . . then what's wrong with us? Why do we have the nightmares?'

'We are reincarnating.' I slid abruptly out of Seth's arms. 'I know you don't believe the legend, but that part at least is true.' I folded my legs under me. 'Let me tell you how I ended up in Mount Hermon.'

When I'd finished the others seemed to be holding their breath. Even the sound of the rain had faded. Then Kyle spoke. 'They really found the bodies where you said they'd be?'

I nodded. 'That's why my parents brought me here.'

Pandra edged away from me. 'You were Jewish?'

I raised my hand to her then let it fall.

'No.' Seth spoke up and his voice sounded strange. He leaned away from me and stared as though I'd grown horns. 'She wasn't Jewish.'

I frowned. 'I was. I was the little girl, Zillah. She was killed in the massacre.'

He raised his eyebrows. 'Really? Quote me something from the Torah.' He looked at me and his eyes contained none of their usual warmth. 'Anything. Go on.'

I stuttered, my mind a blank. 'I-I can't.'

His eyes narrowed. 'That's because you weren't Zillah.'

'Just because I can't quote some stupid religious book!'

His head came up as if I'd jerked him with a string. 'It isn't a stupid book.' His voice held a warning and I blinked. 'I know you weren't Zillah, Cassie.'

'How can you possibly know that?' Anger raged into me.

Why is he doing this?

'I know.' He leaned forward. 'Because *I* was Zillah.'

For a moment I couldn't respond. He might as well have kicked me in the chest. The others looked back and forth between us.

I had to speak. '*Y-you* think *you* were . . . Zillah?'

'I can tell you everything you'd want to know about her life.' Seth spoke bitterly. 'I've been making pretty good progress, apparently.'

'. . . Then who was I?'

Pandra slithered closer to me, like a straying cat returning home for its dinner. 'Don't you see, Cassie?'

Confusion fogged my thoughts. 'See what?'

'You were at the massacre, but you weren't one of the Jews.'

I shook my head, trying to stop the words that were marching towards her mouth.

'You were a Nazi, Cassie. You were one of the murderers.' Teeth showed on Pandra's bottom lip.

I reeled to my feet as rejections smashed across my tongue. 'No!' The initials on the sweet-shop window came back to me. 'K-Kurt.' My hands went to my throat. 'I was K-Kurt Faber.'

A Nazi killer.

Seth's mouth twisted as if he'd sunk his teeth into a lemon. 'All the things you dreamed from Zillah's point of view were things that Kurt saw, weren't they?'

I blinked, recalling Kurt's face in every single vision.

He's . . . right. Everything I dreamed about Zillah was witnessed by Kurt. It's . . . guilt. I'm experiencing her death over and over because of Kurt's guilt.

Hatred surged into Seth's mismatched eyes. 'That's why you aren't afraid of loud bangs and gunshots.' He grimaced. 'Well, I am.' The words '*because of you*' hovered in the air between us, unspoken.

Belinda turned back to me. 'You're afraid of drowning, aren't you? Do you know why?'

I curled my hands into the rug. 'If my dreams are about K-Kurt . . . if that's true . . . I-I think I've seen his death. I didn't know it was him . . . I thought I was Zillah in my last life, but it must have been him, mustn't it?' I choked on a sob. 'He fell down a hill and got caught in barbed wire. H-he drowned in a puddle.'

Seth's legs jerked. 'The man who shot –' he paused and I knew he was about to say 'me' – 'Zillah, drowned in a puddle?'

My mouth filled with the taste of dirty rainwater and I nodded. 'Good.'

I bit my lip hard enough to taste blood and my next words tumbled out unintentionally. 'He knew the Doctor.'

There was a stunned silence and then Pandra's laugh rang out like a series of rifle shots. 'That's stupid.'

'No.' I gestured at the book, which sat between us like a toad on a stone. 'I-I remember . . . Leaza Ashworth was in Kurt's life . . . as Frau Asche. Who knows how many of our other past lives too. I'm sure of it now – she *is* Azael.'

I was surrounded by disbelieving faces.

Finally Lizzie broke the ice-rimmed silence. 'I've dreamed about the Doctor before but I thought it was just real dreaming, you know, *not* memory.' She thrust her drying hair out of her face. 'If it was a memory . . . then she was in Ireland during the troubles.'

Kyle looked at the floor. 'G-Giza, 3200 BC.'

'Does the Doctor gather us together in every incarnation?' I whispered.

Lizzie licked her lips. 'I-if you killed Seth . . . I mean Zillah . . . d-do you think . . . maybe some of us might have, you know, hurt or . . . k-killed each other in past lives?' She was looking at Kyle and her eyes were wide with panic. 'How could we do that to each other?'

Nobody spoke for a long minute. Finally Kyle clenched his fists. 'Oh man, what does she want us to become? . . . Or do?'

Max thumped the sofa. 'That settles it. We can't go back to the Manor.'

* * *

Cold had seeped into the bricks around us and we stared at the floor, unable to reconnect.

Every atom of my body was aware of Seth. He kept a constant distance from me, as if touching me even by accident would stain his skin. Every so often he rubbed his mouth as if to remove the corruption of my lips. I wanted to cry.

'What do we do?' Belinda's voice was tiny.

Seth gestured miserably towards the book. 'I say we take the book to my dad's law firm and let the police sort this mess out.' He got to his feet, still not looking at me. 'We passed a phone in the hallway. If it's still connected, I'll make a call and get him to send someone for us. The Doctor's psychotic; we can't let her damage us any more.' He left the room and out of the corner of my eye I saw Pandra sag.

Her white hair, dried to fluff, no longer poked the sky in defiant spikes. The style now made her look like an old woman rather than a rebellious teen.

If the Doctor treated her like a daughter, how must she be feeling?

I shifted across the carpet until my sodden jeans touched hers. 'I won't leave you,' I whispered. 'You can come home with me.'

She moved her leg so we no longer touched and snorted. 'My choices are pretty limited, aren't they? I'm too old for foster care now.' She turned her back on me, curled up and faced the wall. 'I can't deal with this tonight. I'm going to sleep.'

Seth's low voice murmured through the stone. He must have managed to get through to his dad. Unable to hear individual words I just listened to the rise and fall of his tones.

His dad'll send someone for us tomorrow and I'll never see him again.

In one night I had lost both Pandra and Seth. I felt as if my heart was bleeding into my chest.

It serves me right. I was a Nazi and I deserve to be alone.

CHAPTER TWENTY-ONE
PARTNERS

Gradually the others fell asleep.

I leaned against the wall, unable to close my eyes for fear of what I might see. When Seth saw that I remained awake he groaned under his breath and came to sit next to me, careful not to let any part of his body touch mine.

Finally he broke the near silence. 'I know it wasn't you.'

I looked at him sharply, but his gaze was fixed on his fingers. 'It wasn't you, exactly, but . . .' he tailed off. 'I just need some time,' he murmured. His eyes lifted: confused, angry and lost. 'It helps to know that the guy I see every night didn't exactly live a long and happy life, you know?'

I stared at my knuckles.

'I need to get my head round this.' Seth hugged his knees and I tried to look at him without seeing an overlay of Zillah.

I couldn't. In my eyes it was her long dark hair that fell over his shoulders, her slim fingers that were clasped round his legs.

I pictured the gunshot that had killed her and choked back a wretched sob.

We're both haunted by the death of the same girl.

My back slumped until I was curled up against the wall like an animal in its burrow. There was a lump hidden deep in my jacket: Bunny. I pulled the old toy towards my face and inhaled. The book still sat in the centre of the room and so, like the others, I went to sleep with the light on.

I've never been invited into the library before. My chest is so swollen the buttons of my uniform are creaking. Frau Asche must be pleased with me. I pause to adjust my lapels and check there are no scuffs on my boots, then I knock smartly.

'Herein.'

I push the door open. Frau Asche is sitting in the centre of the room, a large book open in front of her.

Lifting her attention from the text she looks at me. 'You've achieved leadership of the local Hitlerjugend, Kurt.'

I nod and pride sizzles through me.

'I have important news for you.' She rises and walks round

the table. 'The training academy wants you. Do you know what that means?'

The academies were designed to nurture future Party leaders. No one from Hopfingen has ever graduated to one. I'll be the first. I nod vigorously to show my understanding and the Frau smiles. 'You have a great destiny, Kurt, and I will be there to guide you.'

As she turns back to the table I wonder if I can borrow a poetry text and take my chance to peer around the library. However, it is not the books but the large paintings hanging on every wall that capture my attention.

Terrifying religious scenes surround me. In one I see the great flood. The artist has taken pains to focus on the terror of the drowning masses and the pleading in the faces of those who reach for rescue. In the centre of the frame a mother stands hip deep in swirling water. She thrusts her baby towards Noah but his arms remain resolutely crossed.

Distressed, I turn from that painting to another, which shows what appears to be a giant, forging through the flood water, a bull on each shoulder. His face is grimly determined as he heads for higher ground through the rising foam.

Yet another piece of art shows an angel, his wings being torn from his back, his legs and shoulders in the process of being pinned to the night sky.

'Kurt.' I snatch my attention from the paintings and return it to the Frau. 'There is just one thing I am not happy with. Reports of cruelty to the younger members . . .' Her voice trails off.

I blink. Surely she isn't serious? Such things are encouraged, to weed out the weak, but I'm a fair leader to the younger boys; I don't indulge in unnecessary cruelty. Who's been saying otherwise?

'I-I don't know what you mean,' I stammer.

'Exactly,' she snaps. 'A future leader of the Nazi party needs to be hard, to make his men strong. I've been working with you for some time now, Kurt, and I don't see any evidence of the strength that a leader needs.'

'I . . .'

She slams her hand on the book. 'We've talked about this, Kurt. If you want the dreams to leave you, you need to indulge the creatures plaguing you. The more you ignore them, the harder they will work for your attention and you know what that means.'

I catch my breath and my reflection distorts in the shine of my black boots. 'What must I do?'

The Frau licks her lips. 'When I get back from my next trip to

Berlin I'd like to hear that you have been nurturing strength in the other boys. Cull the weak. They have no place in Germany.'

I didn't sleep the night through, none of us did. Every so often I'd jerk awake, heart pumping, convinced the Doctor was about to burst through the door.

Then there were the times we were all woken by the sound of another of us deep in the throes of a nightmare. Each time a scream or sob shattered my sleep I moved to comfort the dazed dreamer and by the morning we had all relocated into a huddle with the sofa as a base. Yet even in the confusion of the huddle Seth was careful not to let his limbs touch mine.

Eventually I was pulled out of my nightmares by a yank on my right arm.

My eyes shot open and I raised my fists, prepared to fight for my freedom. I blinked away the blurry detritus of the night and, when I could see clearly, realised it was Seth who held me. My heart lurched.

His hair was messy from sleep but his eyes burned.

'What is it?' I struggled to sit, lifted my head from Lizzie's leg and moved Kyle's shoulder from my left arm. The other two rolled over, but didn't wake. I glanced at the window. Daylight was yellowing the curtain edges. 'Is it the Doctor?'

Seth shook my elbow. 'Pandra's gone.'

'Gone?' I looked, as if I'd find her somewhere in the pile. Then I realised someone else was missing. 'Where's Lenny?'

'Do you think she's gone back to the Manor?' Belinda combed her hair with her fingers.

Lizzie's gaze darted into the dawn shadows that edged the room. 'What I don't get is – why did she take Lenny? They're not exactly natural partners, you know?'

Max nodded. 'She hates Lenny even more than the rest of us.'

A distant thought was nagging at me. Something about what Lizzie just said: *they're not natural partners.*

My fingers fumbled in the pocket of my jeans. There I found the paper Seth and I had lifted from the Doctor's notebook. At the bottom I read the words '*Natural partnership with Grand Dragon*' and I frowned.

'Does anyone know what a Grand Dragon is?' I barely asked it out loud but the room quieted around me, silenced by the strangeness of my whispered question.

'I do.' It was Max. 'Why?'

I passed the paper over to him and he read the smudged print with a frown.

'We found it in the Doctor's office.' I explained.

'Let me see.' Belinda's tone had Max wordlessly passing the paper on, but his eyes, for once, were elsewhere.

'What does it mean?' Seth prompted him.

'You guys have never heard of David Curtiss Stephenson?' Max shuddered as he read the name indented on the top of the paper, and his American accent seemed stronger than usual.

I shook my head; we all did.

'We studied him in history class last year.' His fingers worried at a button on his jacket. 'The Doctor thinks one of us was Stephenson?'

'Max,' I snapped. 'Who was he?'

'Is this important?' Lizzie had the paper. 'If the Doctor is on her way, shouldn't we leave and talk about it later?'

I was about to agree, but Max reached across Belinda and gripped Lizzie's arm. 'Lenny's missing so this is important.' He swallowed and released her. 'If one of them . . . no, it'll be Pandra.'

If Pandra was Stephenson . . . Well, he was KKK.'

There was a shocked silence then Belinda tossed her head. 'You mean Ku Klux Klan right? Well, duh, Lenny isn't black, so why would she hurt him?'

Max sighed. 'It wasn't just African Americans that the Klan didn't like, Bel. And David Curtiss Stephenson was a Grand Dragon.'

Seth frowned. 'What does that mean exactly?'

'A Grand Dragon was the head of the KKK for a state. Stephenson was head of *twenty-three* states. He was like *the* Grand Dragon. Just in Indiana he got the membership to about . . . three hundred thousand people.'

'What happened to him?' As I leaned forward Seth raised his eyebrows. '*Something* must have happened to him, or Pandra wouldn't be here,' I explained.

Max nodded. 'Cassie's right. There was this woman, Madge Oberholtzer.' He refused to look at any of the girls. 'Stephenson kidnapped . . . and raped her.'

'What?' I sat bolt upright, remembering Pandra's room, filled with pictures of a tormented woman. *She's called Madge something.* I looked pleadingly at Max. 'Then Pandra might not be Stephenson.

She told me she *stopped* Madge from shooting herself.'

He shook his head. 'Madge Oberholtzer did try to shoot herself. When Stephenson stopped her she took poison.' He looked me right in the eye. 'His prison sentence started the decline of the KKK. He died in 1966.'

Seth's voice jerked me back into the here and now. 'He's got Lenny.'

I blinked. 'You mean *Pandra* has him.'

'Pandra isn't herself. She's been in the Doctor's control for longer than any of us. Right now she's probably more Stephenson than she is Pandra.'

Lizzie's usually sunny face was haunted. 'He sounds more evil than my past lives put together.'

Seth nodded and did not look at me.

'*Close to emergence*,' Kyle whispered. 'Oh man, that's what the paper says. Close to emergence.'

'That must mean Stephenson is close to taking complete control of Pandra,' I whispered.

'So Pandra's taken Lenny back to the Doctor?' Belinda looked confused.

'No.' Max shook his head, half bowed. 'That's not Stephenson's

M.O. She's taken him somewhere to punish him.'

Immediately my thoughts flashed to Pandra's secret place.

Surely she wouldn't take Lenny back there: it's the first place I'd look.

'We have to split up.' I sat straighter. 'I'm going to search the woods around the Manor. I have a feeling she might have gone back there.'

I can stop her, whatever she's doing. If the others find out about her secret place, they'll never forgive her. They'll want to leave her with the Doctor.

Seth nodded. 'The woods are a big place. I'll help you search them.' He gestured at the others. 'You guys pair up and look around the farm and dale. Don't do anything risky. My dad's sending people to pick us up at midday so we need to be back here by then.' He gauged their subdued faces. 'Okay?'

Quietly the others paired up.

'We'll take the road towards the village,' Belinda said, and Max nodded.

Kyle shrugged. 'Lizzie and I'll take the farm and fields.' He turned to Seth. 'What if we find her?'

Seth was tying his hair firmly into an elastic band. 'Then one of you better stay with Lenny while the other goes for help. Do what you have to with Pandra.'

Kyle and Max looked at one another, eyes narrowed, and I shivered. For Pandra's sake I hoped I'd find her first.

Outside nothing stirred but wisps of mist that clung to clumps of mud. As we crept out of the kitchen door a crow shot up from a dip with a whirr of feathers and a raucous cry.

I wanted to reach for Seth, but didn't. My touch would probably make his skin crawl.

Soon our trainers pounded on dew-dampened tarmac. I tried to match my pace to Seth's; despite the trees lining the road I felt exposed. 'Should we be walking in the open like this?' Anxiously I looked ahead.

Seth pointed at a rise of rock to our left. 'We don't have time to navigate that.'

I looked. To either side of us the terrain was crumpled like one of my old art projects. Mossy patches looked as if they'd fall apart under our feet and boulders stuck out of hillocks like bad teeth.

Seth checked the sky, where the dawn had just finished

pinkening the horizon. 'There shouldn't be anyone around this early. If we hear a car, we'll just have to try and hide.'

I stared around. The idea of hiding was laughable. Even distant sheep appeared like exclamation marks on the black hills. I stuck my hands into my pockets and hurried.

We made it to the outskirts of the Manor grounds without being seen. There was no movement on the long driveway and the only sounds were the piping calls of birds.

'We should split up.' I cast a glance at Seth, half hoping he'd insist on staying with me, but he nodded his agreement.

'I'll check around the rest of the grounds then follow you into the wood.' His hands moved over the book stashed in his jacket.

I gestured at his coat. 'Maybe we should hide it.'

'In case I'm caught, you mean.' Seth nodded. 'Here then, behind the sign.' He tugged the grass back to find a crack in the earth then shoved the book into the ground. He glanced at his watch. 'If I don't catch up with you in the woods, meet me here at eleven. If I don't make it, you'll have to get the book to my dad.' He pulled a stiff rectangle from his coat pocket. 'That's his business card.'

Careful not to touch him I took the offering.

'Good luck.' He dug his fists into his jacket, turned on his heel and disappeared into the undergrowth.

'Be safe,' I whispered.

Alone, I headed towards the woods.

There was open space between the new range and the trees. I crouched behind a holly bush and watched the Manor for signs of life.

The Doctor has to have realised we're gone by now.

I squeezed my eyes closed. *Why didn't I tell Seth where Pandra's secret spot is? If I'm caught, there'll be no one to help Lenny.*

My jeans were soaked through, but I still didn't dare move. I only had to cross one hundred yards but it was in full view of the rec-room window, the one with my initials carved into the sill.

If I'm seen, I'll just have to run like mad and hide in the woods.

After one final check around I forced my legs into the starting position, lifted my fists to my chest and sprinted on to the lawn.

My feet pounded almost silently on the grass, but the beating of my heart sounded like a message drum calling, 'Here I am – come and get me.' I ducked my head, trying to run faster.

The damp made the lawn treacherous and my feet slid out from under me. With a single indrawn breath I skidded and my elbows hit bark. I'd made it to the trees. I landed on my back and rolled till I was hidden behind a silver birch. Then I looked back at the Manor.

My eyes created figures out of the morning mist. I had to blink several times before they cleared and I realised there was no one chasing me.

Picking my way over fallen branches I tried to remember the route Pandra had taken to the cave. All the time I was listening for Lenny, but the woods were soundless and the deeper I got the more the undergrowth seemed to suck the noise from the world.

Above me the greenery thickened and trees seemed to twist in my direction as if trying to drive me back. I huddled deeper into my jacket and eventually let my fingers seek the comforting lump that was Bunny.

Crack.

The surface gave way beneath my right foot and something lashed towards my face.

Instinct took over and I threw myself backwards. Pain

lanced beneath my eye, but I crashed into a log before it could register properly.

The landing stole my breath and for a long moment I lay still, smothered in a blanket of hurt. Then I felt my chest. I didn't think my ribs were broken so I sat up carefully and explored my throbbing ankle. As I felt for a sprain my face started to sting. Something wet and warm tickled my cheek.

I'm bleeding.

My probing fingers discovered a slash that ran from the top of my nose almost to my ear.

What did this?

Stunned, I looked down. There was a hole in the ground where my foot had been.

Inside the hole was some frayed string and around it broken sticks were splayed like ribs at an autopsy. It looked as though someone had covered a hole with sticks and grass so that it wouldn't be seen. Above me a branch was bent out of shape. Dangling towards me, the whip-like end dripped with my own blood.

Suddenly I heard Pandra's voice again: 'if you want to come here, it's best you come with me.'

This trap had not been meant for a hare. I drew in a shuddering breath. Pandra had meant to injure anyone wandering in the woods. I didn't know if she'd set the ambush long ago, or if she was expecting me to follow her today; either way, the reckless violence of her actions squeezed my chest like giant hands.

Trembling, I pushed myself to my knees and then to my feet. I had to go on. Tentatively I tested my right foot. Agony stabbed towards my knee, but it bore my weight.

At least this tells me Pandra can't be far.

There were two more traps on my route. Once I knew what to look for they weren't too hard to spot. One I tripped with a branch poked into a pile of leaves, another I managed to sidestep. Either might have crippled me. Although I was using a slow pace I was panting as if running a marathon. My eyes burned with the effort of checking every step, so when the ground in front of me vanished I had to pinwheel my arms to prevent myself from stumbling down the slope.

For long moments I stared at the incline. I'd been putting off the thought of it, but now had to accept that I would have to go down that hill.

I know the Doctor said the Manor grounds didn't flood . . .

but there was a stream down there once . . . and the storm last night was a bad one.

Suddenly I was hit by an attack of vertigo. I bent over double, retching violently.

Weg vom Hang!

I fell to my knees clutching my head.

Weg vom Hang!

'Kurt! Th-this isn't the slope you died on. Let me do this.' I tried to get to my feet.

Nein.

My head pulsed with a headache that almost blinded me and I pressed the fingers of my left hand into my eyes.

'I have to go down there.'

Das mußt du nicht.

An image of no-man's land flashed in front of my eyes like a strobe.

'This isn't the same,' I cried desperately. 'There's no barbed wire on this hill. It isn't raining. We aren't at war.' I staggered one step forward.

Du bist dumm, wenn du meinst, es gibt keinen Krieg.

'It's not that sort of war.'

My head felt as if spikes had been rammed through it and nausea slashed at my stomach with clammy claws.

I swallowed.

Maybe . . . maybe I don't have to go down there. Lenny might not even be in the cave.

Ja. Weg vom Hang!

As I started to move away from the hill the wind whipped a blizzard of leaves into my face and I stopped.

I can hear Lenny.

He was crying for help; and he was somewhere at the bottom of the hill.

CHAPTER TWENTY-TWO

TRAPPED

Before Kurt could stop me I inched my left foot on to the slope. As I tilted downwards my ears rang with the screaming of a panicked German.

Images flashed into my head, stronger than before. They mingled with the scent of blood from my own injury and made Kurt's death scene completely real.

My feet slip and the ground isn't there to catch my fall. I howl as I roll down a steep hill.

Still at the top of hill I fell into a crouch and dug my left hand into a patch of moss. It wasn't a particularly good handhold, but it reminded me of where I was, and when.

My chin knocked into my chest as I fought for breath. 'There's a little boy down there who needs me.'

Ein erbärmlicher Schwächling.

A pathetic weakling.

'A ten-year-old boy. Let me help him.' I stood up, swaying. The only way down this slope was quickly. I'd just have to hope Pandra hadn't booby-trapped my descent because I wasn't going to be careful.

Nein.

'Yes.'

Deliberately I sent my balance into the wind. If he didn't want to fall, Kurt had to let me move. My twisted right ankle took all my weight; I cried out and staggered on to my left foot. With fear closing my lungs, I pelted down the slope, stones flying. I had no choice.

The bottom of the slope arrived shockingly fast. As the ground levelled I stumbled and nearly lost my footing. Finally I tottered to a standstill. Straggling pebbles bounced around me for a few seconds, then stopped.

I hauled in a breath and despite the blood that crashed in my ears I heard the faint caw of a boy's cry.

I did it.

For a moment I allowed dizziness to overwhelm me. Then I

forced myself to start limping along the dry stream bed.

I stopped outside the bush that hid the cave and tried to think of a plan.

Pandra won't be happy to see me.

Cursing, I looked around. The area was empty of anything I could use to defend myself.

Then my eye fell on the bush.

Thorns dug into the skin of my palm but I ground my teeth and continued to twist. Finally I managed to wrench off a fairly hefty limb.

If Pandra comes at me, at least this will give her something to think about.

I gave my weapon an experimental swing, took a deep breath and stepped into the darkness.

Pandra looked up. The torch was balanced on an outcrop above her head and she was sitting cross-legged in its circle of light. 'I wondered if you'd come,' she said. 'I wasn't sure you'd make it down the slope, though, not after last time.'

I grimaced and continued to walk towards her.

'Did you come alone?' She cocked her head. 'Or were the others delayed by my little surprises?'

Anger made me raise my weapon. 'I came alone, Pandra, sorry.' I looked around the cave. I'd expected to see Lenny somewhere nearby, perhaps even tied up, but there was no sign of him. 'Where's Lenny?'

Pandra ignored my question and gestured for me to sit on the rug beside her. 'I knew you wouldn't let me down. We're so alike.' The light glinted from her teeth as she smiled. 'Just like sisters. Isn't that what you want, for us to live together as sisters?'

My jaw sang as I gritted my teeth. 'It could work. Come home with me and we'll find another Doctor.'

Pandra shifted her hands into her lap. Her rings glittered. 'There isn't another Doctor. Anyone else will say we're crazy.'

Carefully I stepped into the halo of light that surrounded her. 'Then we'll help each other.'

'Yeah, right.' Pandra sniffed derisively.

'Come on – just having someone else understand will help and maybe we can learn how to do what the Doctor *should* be doing.'

Pandra licked her lips. 'I don't have time for that,' she murmured.

'Why not?' My toes reached the edge of the rug.

Pandra touched her forehead. 'You *don't* understand then.' She cocked her head like a bird. 'He's right here. I can feel him.' Her voice lowered and her final words were in the tones of a frightened little girl. 'I'm slipping away.'

Before I could answer her, I heard Lenny again and this time he was calling my name.

I peered around the cave, but no movement shifted the shadows. I lunged and grabbed the torch with my free hand. Pandra didn't even try to stop me. I swung it round, pointing the beam at every lump I could see. The light showed me nothing but rock.

'Lenny?'

I circled and my trainers thumped on the floorboards. A horrible suspicion took hold of me. 'Pandra, you *didn't!*'

I threw the branch aside and hauled planks from the grave hole. Directing the torch towards the depths I tried not to look as the light swirled c _ ~ corpses heaving with ants and maggots. The glow barely touched the blackness beneath the uppermost ledge. 'Lenny, are you down there?'

'H-help.' His voice was hoarse; he'd been screaming for ages. I wasn't surprised.

'I'm going to get you out. Can you come into the light?'

'Th-they'll g-get me . . . th-the animals.' His reply was barely a whisper, but I understood him and my heart contracted.

'Lenny, they can't hurt you. Come towards the light.' I glared disbelievingly at Pandra and she carried on watching me, expressionless.

Finally I caught sight of movement in the hole and directed the torch beam as best I could. Lenny was cowering at the very bottom of what looked like a ten-foot drop. His face turned to mine. Tears had tracked lines into the dirt that smeared his cheeks.

'I need a rope.' Automatically I cast the beam around and Lenny gave a squeak as the light shifted from him. Quickly I directed the glow back and turned to Pandra. 'How'd you get him down there? Where's the rope?'

Her lips twitched. 'What rope?'

'Then how . . .' I stopped.

She just shoved him in.

Quickly I pushed the horror from my head. I had to stay strong. 'Lenny, are you hurt? Is anything broken?'

His voice shook tearfully and the whiny tone that usually

drove me mad was gone. 'I-I think I've sprained my ankle . . . and my wrist hurts.'

Pandra leaned against the wall of the cave. 'Why d'you care? He's pathetic. Leave him down there.' She shrugged. 'It'll do him good.'

'Holy . . .' I smothered my response and wheeled back to the hole. 'I'm thinking, Lenny, alright.'

He whimpered like a whipped dog and inside me Kurt sneered. Fiercely I pushed him to the back of my mind. Then I remembered Bunny.

I pulled the toy from my jacket and his ears flopped comically. I stroked his nose with my thumb and took a deep breath. 'Lenny, I'm going to throw something down to you. It might help. Can you catch?' I swallowed. 'His name's Bunny.'

Beside me Pandra snickered, but I ignored her. I took careful aim and half threw, half dropped Bunny into the hole. Dirt puffed as he landed. Lenny hadn't even tried to catch him.

Feiger hund.

Cowardly dog.

'Shut up.' I closed my eyes for a second to orient myself, then bent over the hole so I could see better. 'Lenny, that's Bunny next to you. Pick him up for me. He's special. He'll look after you while I think.'

Slowly the boy's fist closed round Bunny's leg and drew him in. He kept his face turned towards me, but brought Bunny up underneath his chin, just as I used to. 'There you go. Hold on.'

I turned to Pandra. 'How do I get him out?'

'Get him out?' She looked genuinely confused.

'You weren't going to just leave him in there . . . were you?' But even as I said it I knew the answer. I rubbed my hand over my face. 'This has gone far enough. We have to fix this. The Doctor's poisoning our minds.'

If anything, Pandra relaxed even more and her casual attitude prompted the voice in my head.

Just leave him there. The opfer. *Teach him a lesson.*

'Shut up.' This time I almost screamed and the torchlight jumped as I punched the air, unable to silence Kurt's voice.

Pandra's lips twitched and she leaned forward as if scenting a delicious waft. 'You are pretty close to where I am, aren't you? Can you feel him, just there.' She tapped her forehead just above her right eye. 'Lenny's weak. He doesn't deserve to be called a man.'

'You're right, he isn't a man . . . He's a boy. A scared little boy.' I spat the words through gritted teeth but, against my will, my left foot inched towards the wall. Tendons in my neck ached as I fought for control of my own swaying body. 'You don't believe this, Pandra,' I rasped. 'It's Stephenson talking.'

Her shoulders jerked. 'How do you know about Stephenson?' Then she waved her hand. 'It doesn't matter. I've been trying to tell you . . . there isn't any difference between us any more – I am Stephenson. I'm going to take over where he left off.'

'That's not going to happen,' I lied. Already I knew how easy it would be to let Kurt's beliefs just take me over. His revulsion for Lenny was tearing me apart.

Then I remembered something. Kurt was drawn towards Stephenson because of their shared hatreds: a Grand Dragon and a Nazi, natural partners. But he was in my head and I knew there was more to Kurt than that. With a massive effort I forced my body to swing round and, with a silent apology to Lenny, lifted the torch from his face and held it on the bodies of the animals ranged on the upper ledge.

'There.' I tossed the word towards the presence that lurked behind my eyes. 'What do you think of that?' I forced myself to look at the remains, which revealed Stephenson's love of pain. The rabbits had ligature marks on their legs and necks; the remains of the terrier were burnt.

Every part of me united in revulsion.

Swiftly I placed the torch on the edge of the hole and removed my jacket.

I didn't stop there. I stripped off my cardigan, my thick shirt and my T-shirt. I kicked off my trainers and unzipped my jeans. Finally I stood shivering in my underwear.

'What're you doing?' Pandra frowned.

'Making a rope.' I knelt before the pile and lifted my jeans and shirt. I tied one arm of the shirt to the jeans, fingers fumbling as I worked the material into a large knot. Then I did the same to link each item of clothing.

Pandra held out her hand. 'Wait.' Her eyes glittered wildly in the drifts of light that swept into the cave. 'Don't do this. It's an opportunity for you as well.'

My eyebrows shot up. 'An opportunity for what? Juvie?'

Pandra shook her head. 'The little crybaby ran away last night with the rest of us, they'll all testify to that. You can say you thought he was with me, but that you found me alone. Everyone will think he went off on the moor by himself. This is my secret place. No one will ever find him.'

She's thought it all through.

My skin pimpled and not just because of the cold; it wanted to crawl round to the back of my spine.

I cast a glance towards the hole where Lenny waited to hear his fate.

'Pandra . . .' I began, but she stopped me with a jerk of her hand that I could barely see.

'Listen,' she spoke urgently, her eyes shining now with near-religious fervour. 'Every time I kill something my dreams get easier. They aren't gone yet, but that's because I'm only killing dumb animals. If you join me, your nightmares won't be so bad. I promise.'

I remained crouching, but made no move towards my make-shift rope.

'Don't you want that?' she wheedled. 'I know I do. I want to make the nightmares stop and this'll do it. The Doctor told me.'

I clenched my fists. 'The Doctor can't be trusted.'

Pandra shook her head like a dog shaking off water. 'I thought about it all night and all I know is if she's found a way to take the nightmares away I don't care what she really wants from us . . . or who I have to become.' She started to slide across the floor like a gorgon on a serpent's tail. 'It's working, Cassie. Don't you want to lead a normal life? Isn't that why you're here?'

A shudder rippled through me and I heard a faint whisper.

I shook my head. 'Not like this.'

CHAPTER TWENTY-THREE

FREEDOM

Suddenly a familiar voice shattered the silence. 'It seems we're having a party.'

Pandra's teeth flashed white. 'I thought you weren't coming.'

Pandra told me the Doctor didn't know where this place was. She lied.

I felt like a hare in one of Pandra's traps. Hoping the two of them would be distracted for a moment I groped behind me for the dropped branch.

If the Doctor is Azael, what use is a branch going to be?

Yet as my fingers closed round the club my confidence bloomed. It wasn't a 98k, but part of me knew what to do with it. I drew my arm towards me as the Doctor stalked into the space, bringing in with her a deeper darkness.

'Good morning, Cassie.' She moved to the highest part of the cave and unfolded. Dust shimmered on to her shoulders as her head brushed the ceiling.

I tightened my grip on the stick. 'We have to get Lenny out of the hole,' I whispered.

The Doctor's eyes glimmered. 'You put the boy in the hole, Pandra?' Her tone wasn't censorious, but curious, as if Pandra had performed an interesting trick. 'Well?' she snapped.

Pandra cringed. She looked just like a dog; her whole body strained to go towards her master for a pat.

'How were you going to kill him?'

I blinked. A naive part of me had hoped the Doctor wouldn't actually let any of us die; after all she thought we were Shemhazai's sons. Her words drowned that hope and, despite the chill, sweat dampened my bare skin.

Pandra edged towards the Doctor. 'I thought if I left him down there it would last longer. I figured the longer it lasted the better my nightmares would get.'

The Doctor pressed her fingers together as if she still sat behind her desk. 'Interesting.' She nodded in the direction of the torch-lit depths. 'You came up with this by yourself. You are very close to complete emergence.'

I repeated myself like a damaged doll. 'W-we have to get him out of the hole.'

The Doctor turned to me. 'I think not . . . Let's leave him there and see what happens. We'll need another subject, however: one to torture. Then we can compare results.' Her eyes burned into mine and my heart raced. Then she laughed. 'I wouldn't do that to you, Cassie, you're progressing remarkably well.'

Pandra completed her slither to the Doctor's side. 'She was a *Nazi*, Doctor.'

The Doctor sucked air through her teeth. 'She's accepted it then?'

Pandra nodded.

'Interesting. Kurt is also very close to the surface.' She looked at me like a subject on a lab bench. 'Your break-out means there is a clutch of children who have made significantly less progress wandering around on those dangerous moors. Lenny is already missing; if another disappeared, I'd be blamed for my lax security, but nothing more.'

I gaped and the Doctor turned to Pandra. 'I'll take Cassie back to the Manor. She'll be confined to her room while she undergoes treatment. You can continue here with your experiment and I'll send the nurses out to bring back one of the others.' She turned to me. 'See? The party's just beginning.'

'No.' I lifted the branch like a shield. 'I won't go with you . . . We know what you are.'

An expression of benevolent confusion crossed the Doctor's face. 'What am I?'

'W-we found your book.'

The Doctor hesitated and for a second her poise cracked. Her fists clenched. 'My book?'

'Yes.' I took a deep breath. 'Azael.'

The strange syllables dropped like rocks into the heavy silence. Then the Doctor spread her hands. 'You think I'm *Azael*? My dear, that book is a work of fiction, nothing more.' Her laugh shivered in the dank air. 'You do need my help. Come back to Mount Hermon and we'll talk.'

'I won't go anywhere with you. Your *therapy* is destroying us.'

The Doctor looked disappointed, as if I was behaving like a stubborn child. 'You took part in that experiment; you know my techniques work.' She leaned down. 'Consider how well you'd sleep if you joined Pandra. Wouldn't you like some rest?'

My head ached terribly. God, I was tempted. The branch vibrated as an irresistible wave of dizzy exhaustion washed over me. In the hole Lenny whimpered and my dislike for him spiked.

Why shouldn't I use him to save my own sanity?

But then I thought of Seth.

What would he think if I didn't try to help Lenny? And what about me? If I don't help Lenny, his death'll haunt me just like Zillah's.

I lifted my head. 'Pandra . . . she's trying to turn us into killers.'

The Doctor tutted. 'You know, Cassie, I don't *have* to keep you alive. You can join Lenny in the hole.' She licked her lips then continued. 'I can get you in your next life.'

My heart skipped as if her words had electrocuted me. The Doctor had as good as admitted she was Azael.

I tightened my fist round the branch. 'You might not find me again,' I muttered desperately.

'Oh, I'd find you. Each lifetime you're drawn together.' She leaned towards me. 'And once I've used the dreams to identify you I'll pit you against your brothers, just as I always have, until only the strongest remain.' Her smile made me feel as if I was drowning in sewage. 'Oh, don't worry, Cassie, you're almost always one of the last sons standing. One lifetime very soon you'll be strong enough to do my work.'

Only willpower was keeping me crouching upright. My legs

trembled. 'But there're only eight of us. The book said there were two hundred sons.'

'Then there are only eight of you at this stage. Right now, of course, you have older siblings operating elsewhere.' She showed her teeth. 'A number of you died in Iraq. Some of you are too young to come to me yet, others are on their way.' In the darkness her perfect face was demonic. 'You would have met them over the course of your life.' Her smile widened. 'If you had any left.'

I'll be starting all over again. She'll be able to make me into whatever she wants. I won't recognise her . . . or Seth, or Pandra. Maybe next time he'll be the one to hurt me. Or I might kill him again.

No.

My arm moved and I swung my weapon towards her legs. '*Also bitte.*' Take that.

The Doctor screeched as the branch connected with her right shin. I pulled back and blood splashed into the dust. But before I could raise my hand again, Pandra landed on my back.

'You're ruining everything,' she snarled.

I screamed, dropped the weapon and tried to throw her off. We both rolled towards the hole.

'Cassie?' The voice penetrated the booming surf of terror in my ears.

It's Seth.

Relief snatched my attention and Pandra landed a blow on my injured cheek. My head smacked into the floor and the world swam.

I spat blood and tried to wriggle from beneath the bigger girl, but she trapped my wrist against the ground and twisted. I howled as I felt my bones grind together.

She's going to break my hand.

The Doctor rose to her full height and turned towards the cave entrance. 'Mr Alexander, go back to the Manor. You aren't welcome here.'

'I bet.'

Seth ducked into the cave and the Doctor drew a sharp breath. 'I have patients here, Mr Alexander. This is a therapy session.'

Using one hand Pandra gagged me. At the same time she jammed her elbow on to my arm to keep it pinned. Frantically I shook my head; I had to speak to Seth. Finally, brutally, I bit her palm.

Wailing like a banshee Pandra pulled her skin from my teeth. 'Lenny's in the hole,' I choked.

In the dim light the whites of Seth's eyes glowed, and he barged past the Doctor. 'A therapy session?'

Then, with a snarl, Pandra pressed her forearm into my throat and I lost sight of him. Orange stars burst behind my eyes. I couldn't get Pandra off my bruised chest and I couldn't breathe past her weight.

Her eyebrow stud glittered like a supernova. Dreamlike I reached up with my free hand and caught the silver ball. Instantly her eyes widened but I ignored her plea and tugged. Her blood sprayed across my face.

Again she shrieked and Seth pulled her off me by her armpits. I rolled to my knees, clutched my throat and groped for the fallen branch.

'Get Lenny out,' I gasped. 'I made a rope.' I indicated the pile of clothes.

'How dare you!' the Doctor growled. 'Mr Alexander, you might do irreparable damage here. Leave now.'

Ignoring the furious Doctor, Seth went for the pile of clothes. Pandra tried to push it into the hole, but I smashed my weapon towards her hands and she pulled back with a rat-like squeal. The wood splintered on the dry floor and I jumped up. Swiftly I put myself between Seth and Pandra, hoping to protect him until he could rescue Lenny.

The Doctor limped forward. 'Look at me, Cassie. This is an adjustment period. I can cure all of you. *Put the branch down.*'

I didn't want to meet her inhuman stare, yet my eyes were drawn to her face and I shivered with terrified awareness: she was trying to hypnotise me.

But Pandra's attack had left my vision blurred. For a long moment the Doctor stared me down . . . and nothing happened. I gestured with my weapon. 'Back. Off.'

The Doctor spread her hands. 'I can't do that. You're a patient of mine *and* my ward. I have to do what's best for you.' She shook her head. 'You have so much potential.'

At my back I could hear Seth trying to get Lenny to catch the makeshift rope.

The Doctor took a step forward. 'Cassie, if you let me help you, both you and Pandra could soon be resting well at night and using your lifetimes of skill and knowledge to accumulate enormous power. With my support the two of you can do anything.'

'Like you helped Kurt?' The Doctor frowned and I continued. 'He remembers you, you know.'

'That's impossible.'

'I don't think he slept any better after he killed Zillah. If he hadn't felt guilty about her death, I wouldn't be dreaming about it. Would I?'

'He was weak. The human side of him was too strong,' the Doctor sneered. 'All of you are still so weak. Even Pandra suffers nightmares when she should be revelling in her memories.'

Her hand came up in some sort of signal. Urgently I swung my branch but I was too slow and Pandra tightened her arms round my neck. I pulled desperately at her grip, but bowed by her strength I fell to my knees.

The Doctor growled. 'If you don't want my help, then fine. You could have been the greatest of them all. Now only the ghost of your memory will remain, as the nightmare of your next incarnation. And whoever you become . . . he or she will help me.' She bent towards me and her eyes glowed with unholy light. 'Here's something to think about in your last moments. When Pandra's ready the first people punished will be your parents. If I'd had you from the start, you would have been the most terrible of my brother's sons. Nothing would have stood in your way.'

Thank God Mum and Dad took me away from her.

Gratitude to my parents brought out other memories, ones I thought I was losing: learning to spot my own constellation with Mum, watching wrestling with Dad. Suddenly the roaring of blood in my ears reminded me of the WWE arena.

The Doctor's laughter faded as I forced my legs to take both my weight and Pandra's. Grunting with effort I rose to my feet. Then I staggered backwards and slammed her into the wall.

Her arms loosened and as I corkscrewed out of her grip Pandra dropped to the ground. I moved away from her and a tide of dizziness surged through me. For the first time I recognised Kurt's infringement, gave in to it and let him take over.

Kurt kicked Pandra on to her back. Then he raised my arm and jumped, throwing my legs out in front to hammer an elbow drop into her sternum.

Pandra was still trying to move.

'Ach, Nein, Nein.'

He rolled Pandra on to her front and drew her into a Full Nelson, locking my fingers behind her neck. Then he looked up.

The Doctor stood clenching and unclenching her fists, her face ugly with rage.

'*Krüziturken*,' he spat. *Damn you.*

He forced Pandra's head forward, then receded.

I swallowed. 'I can kill her with this.'

'Go on. Then you'll be mine anyway: a murderer. It won't take me long to find Pandra again. What're a few more years to me?' The Doctor stopped an inch in front of me. Her breath heated my face and her eyes shone in the darkness like a tiger's.

'What are you frightened of becoming, Cassie Smith? You already have the soul of a killer.'

Behind me Seth groaned and I heard the sounds of struggle as Lenny climbed out of the hole. 'Lenny, you have to hurry – Cassie needs help.' His tone mixed sympathy and frustration.

Lenny whimpered and, at the sound, my lips arched into a sneer.

'You see.' The Doctor tasted the air. 'You know what you are.'

I shuddered, then Seth's fingers curved round my bare shoulder. The shock of contact curled my toes.

'Cassiopeia, listen to me. You don't have the soul of a killer.'

'I-I do.'

'I know you . . .'

'You *hate* me.'

'No.' His fingers dug into my collarbone. 'I forgive you, Cass.'

'What?' The Doctor fried Seth with her gaze. 'Where's Zillah? She won't forgive so easily.'

Seth inhaled sharply. I tried to turn to him, but didn't dare release Pandra. My heart sank. 'S-Seth?'

Only our panting broke the dense silence.

Finally Seth looked up. 'I *am* Zillah. You'll have to deal with me.'

The Doctor roared and spittle shone on her lips. 'I could give you the world. All of you.'

Seth shook his head. 'What's the point in gaining the world if we lose our souls?'

The Doctor gave a tinkling laugh of genuine humour and shook her head. 'You've read the book and you still don't understand? You children *have* no souls.'

As Seth stiffened, something switched on in my mind like a torch. 'You're right, we did read the book.' I dropped Pandra, stepped over her and craned my neck to look the Doctor full in the face. 'It said Azael couldn't hurt any humans directly.'

I glanced at Seth. 'He's bound by a law, remember?' I turned back to the Doctor. 'That's why you need me and Pandra and the others, isn't it? *You* can't hurt humans but we can.'

'You're very much mistaken.' The Doctor's huge muscles trembled but she still did not raise her fists.

'Cass.' Seth was speaking again. Excitement roughened his voice. 'There was something else in the book. Do you trust me?'

Without taking my eyes from the Doctor I nodded.

'Repeat after me. Our Father . . .'

'What?'

'Do it, Cassiopeia.'

'Our . . . Our Father . . .'

'Who art in heaven, hallowed be Thy name.'

I echoed every word.

'Thy kingdom come, Thy will be done, on earth as it is in heaven.'

Pandra groaned. 'What do you think you're doing?'

The Doctor said nothing, but her eyes burned and there was nothing human in them.

'Give us this day our daily bread, and forgive us our trespasses, as we forgive those who trespass against us.'

'Lead us not into temptation, but deliver us from evil.'

Kurt's voice and mine blended. He knew the prayer even if I did not.

Then abruptly . . . he was gone.

And the weight of a hundred lifetimes went with him.

In a flash I remembered playing a game when I first started school. One of my classmates had held my arms down for one whole minute then released them. Like objects foreign to my body they had risen of their own accord.

Now I felt like that all over and I knew what it would be like to fly.

I came back to myself to hear Seth shouting at the top of his voice.

'Azael is here, Lord.'

And Lenny finished, 'Amen.'

The Doctor reared back. 'You foolish little . . .'

Her face rippled and changed. Azael was shedding his disguise. For a long minute pure panic distorted the inhuman symmetry of his face. Then the features stilled into androgynous calm.

The Doctor's form flickered and disappeared: an image from a burning reel of film. Then wings started to unfurl from the angel's back. They moved awkwardly, the muscles long disused, cracking like the fingers of an old man. Long feathers unfolded and popped into place over the pinions. Beneath the flight feathers appeared a cloud of down so pale and soft my fingers itched to hold it to my cheek.

And to my surprise Azael's wings were white. Pure, unsullied and glowing they showed me that the colour I'd known as white before this moment was nothing but dirty grey.

The space wasn't big enough for Azael to stretch as fully as he needed and he turned back and forth, muscles twitching restlessly to reveal razor-sharp claws on the tip of each wing.

He started to laugh. 'I should thank you, boy; I was buried in that *stinking* human form for millennia, thinking He was still looking for me.' Azael stretched his arms to each side, luxuriating. 'But now I can start it myself . . . the war that really will end all wars! My wait is finally over.'

Stunned, I watched, unable to feel anything but incredulous joy.

'Seth,' I whispered. 'I'm free.'

Then, with a rush, the air was sucked from the cave. I followed it with my eyes just in time to see the bush that had provided me with my weapon burst into flame.

Seth threw his arms round me and bore me to the floor as fire boiled over the ceiling like an exploding gas leak.

'*Holy shit!*' Lenny shrieked, and scrambled to the back wall. He landed next to Pandra, but didn't even acknowledge the presence of the girl who had tortured him.

'No!' Azael screamed as the fire consumed him.

From beneath Seth's armpit I squinted upwards. Inside the suit of licking flame Azael's eyes blazed like black diamonds. The gleaming feathers lost their radiance and downy fluff crackled like popcorn.

Then Azael bent in the middle and was yanked backwards like a toy on a string. His wings snapped against the cave walls and his claws left sparks bright enough to see through the fire as he tried to hold on.

'No!' Azael's wail ululated along the ravine. Swiftly I wriggled from under Seth and crawled after him on bare knees. I emerged into the daylight just in time to see a bright dot speeding into the sky like a reversing comet. Then it melted into the sunlight and was gone.

Seconds later Seth staggered out of the cave, a shell-shocked Lenny in his arms. Then he placed the younger boy gently on his feet. Standing unsteadily, Lenny stared up at the trees with glazed eyes. As he still clutched Bunny in a death grip I decided to leave the toy with him.

Seth frowned at the sky. 'Azael's gone?'

I nodded, dumbly.

'I don't believe that just happened.'

I shook my head and wrapped my arms round my chest. I was torn between trying to cover my nakedness and wanting to cradle my injuries.

Immediately Seth shrugged off his jacket and draped it round my shoulders. The pockets were weighted with what turned out to be my trainers. He'd stopped to pick them up for me.

I pulled the duffel round me like a duvet: my bloodied fingers trembled too hard to fasten the toggles. Then I jammed my feet into my Converse without untying the laces. 'W-where's Pandra?'

'Don't care.' Seth looked at me. 'You look different . . . happy.'

I was. I was aching, bloody and happier than I'd ever known how to be. I raised my arms because language simply wasn't enough. 'Kurt's gone.' I lowered my hands and caught the coat back around me. 'He left before Azael did. But . . . why?'

Seth's lips quivered. 'Cass, you saved Lenny and you prayed for forgiveness. You acted like an angel is supposed to . . . remember?' My mouth fell open and he looked at the hill. 'Come on, it's nearly eleven. We have to find the others.'

'What about Zillah?'

Seth cleared his throat and turned back to me. 'I don't think Zillah will haunt me any more.' He flushed and his fingers met mine in the lightest of touches. 'She moved on . . . when she forgave Kurt.'

The colours around me seemed to brighten, and the breeze lifted the singed ends of my hair. I turned my face into the wind and smiled. For the first time in my life I knew I would sleep well the next time I closed my eyes: deep and dreamless and free.

For long moments I stared at the sky; if Azael really was joining his brother, tonight it would be changed. Bravely I weaved my fingers through Seth's. Now we had to go and tell the others what had happened. We'd have to find out which of them needed to forgive and which needed forgiveness. We'd finally have to hear one another's stories. Then, somehow, we'd have to track down the rest of Shemhazai's children and explain it all to them. Explain that hatred and pain led to an endless cycle that could only be broken in one way: by redemption.

SIX WEEKS LATER

M y fingers hovered over the laptop, ready to write my first email to Seth. We'd swapped addresses before our parents came for us, but I hadn't heard from him.

I'd been waiting for him to make first contact, giving him space to clear his head. I'd needed some time too. Now my imagination filled me with fear. Once clear of the Manor had he changed his mind? Did he hate me again?

I flexed my fingers. What should I say?

I decided to just start writing. I didn't have to send the email when it was done.

Dear Seth

I stopped. Then deleted it. Tried again.

Hi Seth

I wasn't sure whether to send this. You can delete it without reading it if you like.

I'm writing because I need to talk and you're the only one

who understands what's going on with me. I've been in touch with Lizzie and Max. They're still having their nightmares. I wish I could help them.

I've decided to take science and psychology courses for A levels. I want to be able to do what the Doctor should have been doing. I want to actually be able to help any more of us that turn up. The Doctor said we'd meet more sons, that we'd all be drawn together. I hope I can get qualified before that happens.

I reckon I can fast-track through college and uni. It turns out I'm not stupid. You wouldn't believe how my marks changed once I'd actually had some sleep. I seem to just be able to dredge up the knowledge I need from a past life.

Can you do that?

I still have bad dreams sometimes. I guess we'll never forget what the Doctor put us through, but now I can control my nightmares better. They don't consume me.

I have to sleep with the curtains open, though. I need to be able to see the star, to be sure Azael is still trapped up there with Shemhazai. If I can't see it, if I can't check he's still there, the old nightmares come back.

Do you still dream of Kurt and Zillah? You freed the spirit trapped inside me when you forgave me, but that doesn't mean you don't still hate me . . . what I did to you.

The police have been round asking questions. They're looking for Pandra and the Doctor. They think they're together. I don't think they'll find Pandra. I reckon she's gone looking for some of the other sons, the ones the Doctor told us about. I couldn't tell the police that, though . . .

I wish I could speak to you. There's too much to put in a single email.

I'll put my mobile number at the bottom.

I hesitated. How should I end?

Automatically I typed:

Love, Cassie

Then I pressed the delete button and changed it.

Love, Cass

Mum's voice floated up the stairs. 'Cassie, don't forget Dad's taking you to the dojo in half an hour.'

I pulled the uniform over my head and spent a happy moment stroking my new brown belt. Then my phone started to ring.

It was Seth.

ACKNOWLEDGEMENTS

To my amazing editor, Philippa Donovan, and the rest of the team at Egmont whose hard work and advice have helped create something I can be truly proud of.

To my agent, Sam Copeland (RCW), and to Cornerstones Literary Consultancy who guided me out of the slush pile.

To the SCBWI team in charge of 'Undiscovered Voices'.

To Sarwat Chadda (author of *The Devil's Kiss*) who read an early draft of *Angel's Fury*, laughed his head off, and pointed out the value of a heroine with some backbone.

To Rob at ACA Productions for working so hard on my chilling book trailer, to Dave Sheppard for contributing the fantastic soundtrack and to Charlotte Palazzo for my brilliant author photographs.

To my ever-supportive in-laws, Pat and Charles, who in addition to cheerleading and impromptu babysitting services very helpfully speak German.

To my parents, Mike and Mary McCarthy, who raised me to believe I could do anything I set my mind to.

To all my friends, old and new, without whom I would most likely have gone insane long ago.

To the children's godparents (especially Shehnaz, Ricardo and Natalie), and my sister and sisters-in-law Claire, Gill and Ros for your support over the years.

And most especially to Andrew James, Maisie Rose Guinevere and Riley Gabriel Bryson Pearce . . . for being you. One day one of you might even read the book.

Thank you all for everything.

EGMONT PRESS: ETHICAL PUBLISHING

Egmont Press is about turning writers into successful authors and children into passionate readers – producing books that enrich and entertain. As a responsible children's publisher, we go even further, considering the world in which our consumers are growing up.

Safety First
Naturally, all of our books meet legal safety requirements. But we go further than this; every book with play value is tested to the highest standards – if it fails, it's back to the drawing-board.

Made Fairly
We are working to ensure that the workers involved in our supply chain – the people that make our books – are treated with fairness and respect.

Responsible Forestry
We are committed to ensuring all our papers come from environmentally and socially responsible forest sources.

For more information, please visit our website at www.egmont.co.uk/ethical